Edward B. Osborne

Letters from the Woods

Random Rhymes, from 20 to 70.

Edward B. Osborne

Letters from the Woods
Random Rhymes, from 20 to 70.

ISBN/EAN: 9783744716734

Printed in Europe, USA, Canada, Australia, Japan

Cover: Foto ©Andreas Hilbeck / pixelio.de

More available books at **www.hansebooks.com**

LETTERS FROM THE WOODS.

[Editorial Correspondence.]

RANDOM RHYMES,

From 20 to 70.

ANNUAL ADDRESSES,

Written for Press Carriers.

BY EDWARD B. OSBORNE.

POUGHKEEPSIE.

1898.

INTRODUCTORY AND EXPLANATORY.

An explanation is sometimes equivalent to an apology, and therefore not out of place in this opening page. The original intention was the printing of a few copies of this little book for private distribution only. But through an outside suggestion (we must confess not requiring much pressure), a larger edition was decided upon.

These sketches, the work of moments of leisure from confining business occupations, and from larger relief during a few days' sojourn in the outer world, where Nature in comparative solitude, sublime and beautiful in its grand adornments, invites the admiring and reverent gaze — were written only for a timely use, to be buried with it. That they reappear in this form, can find no more plausible excuse than to fall back upon an old plea, that Age grows garrulous — that the veteran, looking back to the sterner conflicts of his life assignments, finds delight in "fighting his battles over," and peaceful mortals who have survived their usefulness are prone to think, what is of mastering memory to themselves of the past must possess interest to others, and plead at least, in the words of higher authority, that "a book is a book although there is nothing in it."

"Letters from the Woods" are portrayals of what the Adirondacks were a third of a century ago, when that now frequented and greatly traveled section of our State was almost a *terra incognita*, to be reached only by long foot tramps. All this has been wonderfully changed through the agency of steam transit and the speed of daily coaches in all directions, furnishing facility of access, and carrying with them all the conveniences and comforts of the most popular fashionable resorts. Locomotives and steamboats now utter their conquer-

ing defiance over natural difficulties, where then the lonely
hunter and angler wandered for weeks, meeting only at rare
intervals venturesome mortals, like themselves, leading for
the time being a hermit life.   Looking back through the long
roll of years, we are impressed with the fact, that of the numerous native guides who directed our course over lakes and
streams, and piloted through the almost pathless forests, all
but two or three sleep from their wonted pursuits beyond
time's awakening.

Of the early efforts at "random rhyme" — perhaps the less
said the better.   They mark in memory a somewhat extended
residence in a historical city of New England — which of old
was a reputed locality of witches and their alleged craft.   But
all the witches we encountered were attractive creations of
flesh and blood, abundantly equipped to foster poetic inspira-
tion in the brain of youthful romance.   To become a subject
of their witchery, had there been no more convenient opportunity of companionship, one would have been content to have
accompanied them on a moonlight "broom-stick" excursion
over the city, and have shared with them a chance of mercy
at the hands of puritanical over-righteousness, as the penalty
of such an ærial feat.

At the first blush, the "Annual Addresses," written for the
carriers of a daily journal, may seem like a short string of
old almanacs — their use, if any, having expired by limita-
tion.   (Incidentally of almanacs and their uses, we will add
what our old citizens will probably remember, that it was a
custom to give a running prediction of the current state of
the weather in *italics* on the margin of a page, and in the
suitable season announcement was made to look out for "*show-
ers, lightning*, thunder," etc.   A rural citizen came into the
town of Barnstable, Mass., one day to attend the "Court of
Common Pleas," which was the almanac announcement for
the day.   Directly opposite it in the weather margin was
the word "*thunder*."   The seeker for knowledge, as to what
sort of weather the day was going to bring, took the whole
line in and dropped the authority with the exclamation: "Good

Heavens! we are going to have a shower of Barnstable thunder!") But this is a digression to ease up a little the work of explanation under this heading. We put in extenuation that these addresses have something to plead for their presence here, if for nothing else, that they serve as chronological indicators of memorable conflicts, not only in the history of our own great national struggle to uphold the legacy of our revolutionary sires, but also as data of warring disturbances among other republics on our own continent, as well as of like occurrences on the other side of the Atlantic. It may be remarked in closing, that the same unsettled conditions and uncertainty of stable regal government still largely prevail, as an echo of the long past, and not yet distinctively promising of the millennial era.

POUGHKEEPSIE, 1893.

FOREST AND LAKE.

WITH THE WOODS AND WATERS.

CHAIN LAKES, ESSEX CO., N. Y.,
August 24, 1856.

From the busy occupations of camp life, I will find time for a hasty sketch of the experience of a few days "roughing it" in a portion of the old forests in the northern part of our State. I locate my epistle at Chain Lakes, upon which, and the neighborhood, a moon's half circle was worn pleasantly down to an early evening's crescent.

I left Poughkeepsie in company with an old friend, who has been an annual devotee on the same pilgrimage for a half a dozen years, and was therefore well qualified to put me through the course of seeing the wilderness elephant.

We reached the end of railroad traveling at Fort Edward. The staging from thence to Glens Falls freshened the recollections of long ago. The coach was full seated, within and without, but faithful to coach custom of yore, there was always room for one more.

At Glens Falls we changed vehicle for the drive to Chester, and from thence after supper to Schroon Lake, a pretty village bordering a fine sheet of water about nine miles in length. Here we formed the acquaintance of one of a family of go-ahead young men, by the name of ROOT, who took us late in the evening, behind a lively team, over a lonely but romantic road, to Schroon River, about nine miles distant, where the senior of the family presided as host. He had just completed a large and comfortable mansion for public uses, where we found very agreeable entertainment for the night. Early on

the morrow we started for a point some thirty miles farther
into the wilderness. Our route for most of the way lay
through the primeval forests, over a corduroy road, the overhanging branches darkening the view, and confining it to a
narrow track. Here and there, at long intervals, a log cabin
in the midst of a scanty clearing, upon which a plot of potatoes
was freshly blooming and a patch of oats still green, and around
whose doorway healthy and rugged looking children were
exercising their bare legs and feet, changed the monotony of
the scene.

Occasionally, through an opening we caught a view of some
of the noted peaks of the Adirondack ranges. Of these sum-
mits, Mount Marcy reaches the highest altitude, rising to the
height of five thousand three hundred and thirty-seven feet
above the level of the sea. We passed both branches of the
Hudson river, our route taking us within about fifteen miles
of its source.

As the shades of evening were coming on, we reached the
end of travel by wheel, and took up quarters with Caleb
Chase, who received us with the hospitality common to the
pioneer's home. The morning brought a change in the method
of travel. For a good six miles we were to shoulder our
packs, and other wood appliances, and trudge over a rock-
paved track, which led us to a shanty in the neighborhood of
Goodenow creek, a celebrated trout stream, where we
"shantied" for the first time on the trip. By the courtesy of
Messrs. CRONKRITE and COLVILLE, of Glens Falls, who had
been engaged in lumbering in this section the previous winter,
we had been put in possession of their comfortable log house.
It had been the home of a large number of log cutters during
the season of that work, and it contained all the culinary conveniences needed, under the circumstances, with the additions
we made to the store. How we struck out new ideas and
forces in the science of cookery, at least to one of the party
engaged in the mystery, need not to be stated. It is, perhaps,
profitable that we should some time be thrown upon our own
resources in matters which are not supposed to belong legiti-

mately to the male gender. It is a sort of helper to a fuller understanding of the moral, at least in a domestic sense, that

" The good we never miss we rarely prize."

Beside taking a bountiful supply of trout, for our two meals in the shanty, our main experience, on a tour of inspection through the adjoining forest, was to surprise a trap set for bear, and to slightly appreciate the scare which bruin must have realized, had he come to his invitation before us. But this is an incident of unwritten history, and the obligation of silence has been faithfully kept for nearly two score years. We are confident the bear never mentioned our poaching on his preserves.

We were obliged to leave our comfortable shanty, sacred to pleasant memories, as it was about three miles to the cluster of lakes where our operations were to be mainly conducted. Early in the morning we started over a blind trail, and, after considerable devious and doubtful exploration, we struck the fifth of the chain of water basins which compose this charming group of the North Woods, in many respects without a peer. After a protracted search we uncovered from its hiding place a serviceable boat, which had been designated for our use by our friends at Glens Falls.

Passing down the lakes the far-reaching vision of uprising mountain ranges was a revelation which will be indelibly impressed on memory. On reaching the second lake, at the foot of which we expected to find our venerable shanty, it was in so dilapidated and dirty condition that we were thrown upon our own resources to settle the question of a night's lodging. In this emergency, while dipping our leather cup in the spring, a half-breed hunter, from the St. Regis region, came suddenly upon us. He carried a rifle and a capacious blanket-pack. Entering into conversation with him, we learned that he had come to the lakes for the purpose of capturing a deer. As he was a foot traveler, we proposed he should return with us to the third (and largest) lake, and, after setting a buoy for lake trout, prepare to take an evening

float with one of us for a deer. This arrangement was satisfactory, and we found Mitchell, as our new companion was
called, quite handy in wood life and hunter-craft. After con-
sultation, it was deemed best to camp out for the night, rather
than try the sleeping accommodation of the old shanty we
had left. Mitchell was accordingly deputed to locate the
ground, which he did upon a bank in a nook of the lake, near
a fine spring of water. With tips of hemlock he soon fash-
ioned our couch, and a rousing fire added liveliness as well as
comfort to the scene. Unrolling his pack he produced the
necessary implements and soon our supper was in a fair way
of meeting ardent expectations. Pronged sticks impaled the
fish we had caught on our upward passage, and they were
broiled to perfection. During our repast Mitchell's tongue
was unloosed and he treated us to a narrative of his experience
in moose hunting in the upper Canada forests. He and a
companion had captured about seventy on the Aroostook the
previous winter, and others he said were more successful.
The moose are destroyed mainly for their skins, which are
worked into moccasins and other articles, and are valued at a
high price, paying the hunter well for his exposure day and
night to the rigors of a northern winter.

Late in the evening the "jack" was lit, and it was decided
that I should accompany Mitchell on my first experience at
"floating for deer." Down the lake we glided, hearing
occasionally in the woods on the banks sounds which Mitchell
pronounced as the footsteps of the game we sought, but no
deer were to be seen. While thus seated in blank expectancy,
a couple of "screech owls," in the upper part of the lake,
commenced a volume of unearthly sounds, which echoed in
prolonged cadence from the mountain side. Mitchell broke
into a quiet chuckle, the only attempt we heard him make
toward a laugh, and remarked: "I guess they are serenading
Slee." It became evident that the evening's cruise would not
contribute to our larder. We returned fruitless to our night's
quarters, and reposed upon our verdant bed, a good fire at

our feet, but nothing but a few thin tree-top branches between our overcoats and the sky.

We rose in the morning feeling fully equal to any toils of the day. Mitchell did not feel satisfied to abandon his search for venison, and he started off alone to hunt the lakes. Late in the afternoon he returned empty-handed, having seen but one far-off deer, and gave up the hunt. We had been successful during the day among the lake trout, and prevailed upon him to take a portion of the fish we had on hand. He informed us that during the day he had discovered a shanty in good condition, near the foot of the second lake, near the old one. We accordingly accompanied him down the lake, and took a friendly parting. The shanty proved to be a protection against wind and rain. It had been built and occupied, we subsequently learned, the previous summer, by Rev. Dr. Todd, from a New England city, who had sought the wilderness for recreation and physical relief.

Fishing for lake trout in these waters is a lively occupation. Our average run was about two pounds — the largest, three and a quarter, though, my companion informs me, they have been captured in this lake, weighing nine pounds.

My companion, nothing discouraged by the failure of the preceding evening, took the paddle at an earlier hour, and we put out again for a hunt. The result proved that he was more expert and sagacious than the descendant of the red man. Our prize of the evening was a farrow doe of large proportions and in fine condition. We also run in shore upon a buck and doe feeding together, but there was no temptation to increase our stock of venison.

The wanton destruction of these beautiful animals is telling materially upon the frequency of their resort to the feeding grounds of the lakes. The killing of them merely to gratify the pride of marksmanship cannot be too strongly censured.

Rain fell nearly all of the day following, and of all days, a constant rainy one, in the forest, is among the dullest. Our primitive cabin, with its unrestricted range for smoke, was convenient, at least, for curing venison. But the quantity of

the latter threatened to exceed considerably the demand even
of two vigorous appetites. We therefore concluded to pack
a portion of it and carry it to a shanty on Cedar river, about
three miles distant, whose inmates my companion had previously visited. Slinging our budget on a pole resting on our
shoulders, we took a blind trail single file through the forest,
and were welcomed at the clearing of our lonely neighbors
with a cordiality that made us immediately at home. It was
occupied by Conklin Noxon, whose ancestors, he informed
me, were from Dutchess county. We found him in harvest-
work. He had gathered about twenty tons of hay, and was
preparing to get in his oats, which looked large and heavy
grained. He expected to gather five hundred bushels of
potatoes this season, and the Adirondack quantity of this
crop cannot be surpassed. The demand for these products is
from the lumbermen and their teams, the former of whom
make the old forests vocal through the winter by the meas-
ured stroke of their axes. This climate grows hardy and
vigorous men, who laugh at the icy rigors of the cold months,
make pork and potatoes their regular fare, and perform an
amount of labor which would wilt shop-nursed laborers.

Cedar river is a rapid stream of considerable width and
depth, emptying into the Hudson, after five or six miles further run. At time of spring freshets, when fed by melting
snows, it rises ten to fifteen feet, and affords the outlet for
lumbermen's winter-piled logs.

But I must close my narrative, already perhaps too much extended to interest the reader. To the jaded and workworn,
these still mountain retreats, with their ever pure and sparkling waters and various excitements to mental and bodily activity in new channels, furnish a genial medicine. Whatever
the exposure, there are no unfavorable results. Body and
mind catch the elasticity and glow of the surroundings. Nor
this only. Nature's grandest manifestations have here an
elixir deeper and more pervading. From her lofty rock-ribbed
heights,

          "The masonry of God,"

her far-reaching forests clothed in varying beauty, and her ever harmonizing voices with the soul's out-reachings, come a teaching not easily forgotten beneath the shortened scope of ordinary familiar avocations.

ON INDIAN AND LEWIS LAKES.

No. I.

NORTH RIVER, *August*, 1865.

Travel by rail furnishes but little of incident. And yet the fact that within the space of four hours you are whirled through from Poughkeepsie to Fort Edward, is an event in itself of such proportions, that nothing but custom takes off the wonder. The only out-of-the-way experience was an over-heated axle of one of the cars, detaining the train half an hour. Getting out to learn the cause of the detention, we found the crowd gathered around the affected place, and men pouring water upon the hissing iron, from which ascended a volume of smoke, to the no little alarm of some of the passengers inside.

Saratoga, of course, received a generous share of the living freight who started with us, and the bustling crowd who stopped within its charmed precincts, hurried off to enter the whirlpool of fashion,— perhaps to realize their expectations.

Glens Falls, over which a sirocco of fire swept but a few months since, has risen in beauty from the ashes. With the active, energetic population of our country, fire destroys often only to lead the way for a new creation, and enhanced property value.

At this place steam has not yet found its occupation as the draft horse of thronging travel. The old stage here rattles off in all its ancient glory, and the art of piling in and packing on the traveling community is understood with a perfection that would have excited the envy of the whips of former days, who always had room for one more inside.

2

At Glens Falls our stage load included no less a notoriety than the celebrated E. C. Judson, better known as Ned Buntline, who had for his companion on a lake and mountain excursion Mr. Whitney, of the New York *Sunday Mercury*. Ned has returned in all his glory from a four years' arduous service in the war, having done active duty in the First New York Mounted Rifles. His employment was mainly as a leader in the scouting service, an occupation for which his forest experience and adventurous temperament admirably fitted him. Moving incidents of fight and flight will make Ned more than ever a companionable hero with his old friends and associates in these wilds. He is bound for his old home at Blue Mountain Lake, or Eagle's Nest, as he has christened it, from which he has been absent since the appeal to arms first awakened his martial fire. He gave us a pressing welcome to go with him to his mountain home, assuring us a hearty welcome, an offer which previous engagements compelled us to decline.

To-morrow we pack horses for a trudge into the farther interior, where the deer contest a roaming habitation with the wolf and a still worse persecutor, man — and where the trout gather and grow in the spring-fed and mountain embosomed retreats. Beyond this point Uncle Sam's mail bags can only be reached by a chance outward-bound pedestrian.

No. II.

Prominent among the grand collections of spring-fed water, for which Hamilton county is noted, are Lake Piseco, Lake Pleasant, Lewis lake and Indian lake. At present date the alderman and myself are located on the Lewis river, or as the common pronunciation here is *Lewy* river, about a mile and a half above the inlet of Indian lake. Our host and hostess are a Canadian Frenchman and his American wife, named Gerard, a courteous couple, who are cultivating a productive clearing in the woods, of more than ordinary size and fertility. They are fully mindful of the apostolic injunction not to be " forgetful to entertain strangers," but whether in the exercise of such hospitality they ever fall upon "angels unawares," is perhaps an idle speculation.

One thing strikes an observer in these wilderness clearings, and that is, the deprivation of social privileges by the women. The first thought is, that habitation and inclination are in harmony with the woman denizens of forest life, but I find that it is rarely so. While making the best of circumstances, and doing much to soften the privations of these secluded homes, their longings for the advantages of community life are strong and enduring, and they talk feelingly of the loss to their children and themselves in their confined existence, and find comfort in the hope of a prospective change. It is possible that a young woman, brought up from the cradle to this narrow sphere, and agreeably mated, may find her affinity without discontent here, but even this is a rare exception.

The township of Indian Lake was established in 1859, and before the war contained a population of about sixty souls. The charms of the battle-field, and the high bounties, drew a number of substitutes from this place, some of whom have returned, others sleep with their comrades where no morning reveille can awake them. The lake whose name it bears is about three miles long and a mile in width. It has been a beautiful sheet of water, with picturesque banks, sloping down, in places, from overhanging mountain peaks of majestic altitude. But the hand of utility has robbed it of much of natural beauty. A capacious dam has been built at its outlet, within a few years, for the purpose of flooding both the lake and the Lewis river, which pours a heavy volume of water at all times into it. The dam is closed in the period of the spring freshets, raising the water from twelve to thirteen feet above its ordinary capacity. This supply serves as a reserved feeder for Indian river, the outlet of the lake, and which bears upon its freshet-swelled bosom, the logs cut by lumbermen in this region. These logs pass into the Hudson or North river, into which Indian river empties, and are borne down by the swollen current, in countless thousands, to Glens Falls, where a large portion of them furnish employment for the extensive saw-mills at that place.

As we have remarked, the operation of this dam is fatal to the border beauty of Indian lake. The settling back of the water has, to a great extent, destroyed the trees and solid ver-dure, which once clothed its banks, and left sterile looking marshes, covered with decayed trees, and emitting a dank and unwholesome odor.

Indian lake has been famous as a common resort for deer, and the surrounding forests still hold them in attraction as numerously as any place in the northern woods. But the huntsmen and their dogs give no peace to these graceful and agile forest rangers, and year by year they are being thinned in numbers. The hound is taken into the mountain covert, and, when the trail is struck, the leash by which he is held is loosed, the hunter returns, and the hound goes bounding after his prey. And here commences a race on the part of the deer for dear life. The hound follows with untiring zeal, ever and anon, as the trail of the deer he has in pursuit freshens upon his scent, sounding his baying bugle, a welcome warning to the listening and panting deer, who, as his pursuer thus indi-cates his point of approach again, "bounding forward free and far," seeks the dense covert in some distant retreat. But though the deer may for the time outstrip his foe by superior fleetness, the latter holds to the chase with greater endurance, and as a last resort, in order to throw his enemy off the scent of his track, the deer takes to the lake or river, where the huntsmen, who know his usual path of flight, are lying in ambush for him. As soon as the deer has made a sufficient progress in the water to prevent his return, they take to their boats, and, by superior progress with the oar, secure the cov-eted game. The number taken in this way in these northern lakes is large, and unless the hound is soon withdrawn from this destructive chase, we shall be compelled to bid adieu to these noble animals.

Indian Lake township has its courts for trying breaches of the peace, as well as more settled places, albeit a competent official has to be sought with much travel. A case of this kind occurred yesterday. A hunter passing through one of the out-of-the-way paths came upon a lonely settler who was beating his wife with a club. The blood was flowing freely from her wounds. The cowardly brute fled at his approach, and as he assisted the poor woman to rise, she besought him to enter a complaint against her husband.

He accordingly did so, after much travel and trouble, but when the case came on before the Justice, the woman would not swear against her husband. She said they had some contention, and he "chucked" her a little, but she guessed she had used some hard words to him; on the whole it did not amount to much, and they would get along well enough if other people would let them alone. The Justice was compelled to dismiss the case for want of evidence, and the reconciled pair started off very lovingly for their shelter in the woods, probably to repeat the same wrangling and "chucking" on the first convenient opportunity. It is but a repetition of an old story of woman's trust and forgiveness, and her patient endurance of suffering rather than to part from a brutal husband. The hunter was satisfied that it was a thankless job to interfere in a matrimonial quarrel, and informed the court that man and wife might fight it out the next time without his meddling with the affair.

Indian lake and its tributaries abound with trout, and it is a pleasant occupation to sit in a boat on the lake and watch them springing at full length above the surface for a passing insect or some floating tempting morsel. The points of intersection of the cold water brooks attract the "speckled beauties," and the angler finds capital sport in throwing the fly and playing them skillfully to land. The Alderman is in his glory, and exhibits the same inventive faculty, patient perseverance and ready resources, which have marked and made his success in the business affairs of life. As he lands one of the finny treasures, as broad as your hand, there is a quiet glow of satisfaction, demonstrative that the exploit was done in the first style of old Walton's art. The pleasurable excitement, the vigorous exercise with the oar, the bracing atmosphere, and the plain but genial food, are doing their beneficial work on weakened muscle and sluggish digestive powers, engendered by sedentary pursuits.

Shut in by lofty mountain ranges and far removed from sources of mental excitement, memory feeds the mind with pleasant and painful experiences. Airy voices come to my ear as returns the hour when —

> 'Neath the folds of the snowy drapery
>   Lieth the form so still and cold:
> O'er the pulseless heart the white hands rest —
>   O'er the pallid brow were tresses of gold ;
> But the waxen lids droop heavily now
>   O'er the hazel shade of the beautiful eye,
> And the lips once ruby are ashen and pale,
>   No more will they smile, no more will they sigh,
> But bravely she crossed the dark river,
>   Nor shrank from its cold rolling wave,
> For though lost to our sight here forever,
>   Faith lighted the gloom of the grave.

These thoughts may be intrusive to the reader, however absorbing to this hour and place. To look within our own hearts, and commune with spirit teachings, there is no place more congenial than the solitudes of Nature.

To-morrow we start for Lewis lake, which to reach will require some ten miles rowing, up the river of the same name.

No. III.

My last left us in preparation for an adventure up Lewis river. The delicacies we laid in for the excursion were, about half a bushel of potatoes, a magnificent chunk of salt pork, a few loaves of bread with an allowance of butter, salt and tea, and last but not least in account, a roll of blankets. Into two small boats we packed ourselves and traps, including a guide for each boat, who acted as oarsmen, and an intelligent-looking dog belonging to them, who was acquainted, by long practice, with the track of deer. Our progress was nearer a "zig-zag" than I ever remember of traveling before. After turning a point, in several instances we found we were "advancing backward," and though pulled by lusty oars we marked our passage on the mountain side by slow gradations. Ever and anon the sweeping wings and long legs of a crane would rise to view, startled from his feeding grounds by intrusive and unusual visitors. Numerous hawks wheeled in graceful gyrations overhead, as if watching and wondering at the scene. Broods of black ducks rose occasionally as if averse to too close acquaintance. Arriving at the forks where Jessup river unites with the Lewis, we threw our lines and caught a few trout of quite moderate dimensions, but better than none, where the prospective of a dinner is bounded only by pork and potatoes. Let us not be deemed to speak disparagingly, however, of this great staple, the culinary department in forest life. We bear grateful testimony to a slice of raw pork, peppered and sandwiched between slices from a loaf, eaten at a temporary halt on a well-packed tramp. Stall-fed epicures may find it difficult to appreciate such a repast, but they will be equally at a loss to realize the active and buoyant existence which an appetite reconciled to such fare promotes.

Jessup river at this junction has long been famous as a trouting ground. But as elsewhere in this region, the extensive drought had greatly reduced its waters, and there was little enticement for delay. As we left the Forks (so called, we suppose, from the union at this point of another small stream), we pushed our way up the Lewis river, now a greatly reduced channel. Our oarsmen were repeatedly obliged to wade and drag the boats over bars and sunken branches, making slow progress. About a quarter of a mile below Lewis lake the Falls commence, against which the oar is useless. The cargo must here be landed, and the boats are borne on stalwart shoulders by a forest path and placed in the lower end of the lake.

Lewis lake lies in the north-eastern part of Hamilton county, and is a water basin of great beauty. Lifted many feet above the overflow of Indian lake, vegetable life grows rank and luxuriant, and forms a fitting casket for so pure a gem. Our boats cleaved the narrow outlet, about a quarter of a mile, a paradise of verdure on either side, when the lake burst upon the vision. Something of the stirring emotions which attend the discovery of explorers where the foot of man is supposed never to have fallen, was felt as our boats rode its waters for a mile and a half to the inlet shore. To us it was new ground, as though struck at once from the mint of creation, without vestige of the presence of fellow-men. But we were soon undeceived as to a supposed sole occupancy. Our boats had scarcely struck the beach, when a young man emerged from the path leading to the principal shanty at the lake. He was soon followed by his companion, both having the unmistakable contour of student life, with the pulpit in view. We learned they had come in that morning, to try the fishing, and they soon left in a boat to cast their lines. We explored the woods, and were fortunate in finding a bark shanty, covered on three sides, with a fire-place constructed of stones in front. Here we piled the logs for our night fire, gathered hemlock bough tips for our bed, and not yet reconciled to pork and potatoes as full fare, entered our boats again and tempted the trout at the inlet. They were in sluggish mood, refusing to rise at the fly, but a few were deluded by the sunken bait, and made captives. Here all the rules of fishermen art were at fault. Our light and delicate trappings, falling noiselessly upon the water, came off second best. A clumsy tackling of one of our guides, falling with a loud splash into the stream, took the only five trout of the evening. We have read somewhere of an illustration by an experienced divine, instructing a younger brother in the ministry how to fish for souls. "Now," says he, "you must imitate the example of the skillful angler in your labors. He does not cast his line with a noisy rough throw, as if saying to his expected prey, ' bite or be d———d,' but gently extends the enticing morsel, and wins them to his embrace." Our case, at least, was an exception to this rule. The biggest fish was caught on the other style, after a *ke-chunk* of a heavily loaded line. On returning, we overtook our student acquaintances, and on comparing notes we found they had not taken a scale, and a repetition of the same luck in the morning induced them to abandon the lake in disgust.

Night in the wilderness, with the bright broad canopy above, seen through the interlacing branches of majestic trees, has a charm all its own. As the heavily-logged fire snaps and crackles, and the tree tops are rustled by the breeze into majestic symphony, sleep holds itself aloof, and the mind wanders, quickened to unwonted activity by the surroundings Occasionally the melancholy scream of the Great Northern Diver, from the bosom of the adjacent lake, or the "tuwhit—towho-o-o," of the night owl, familiar to these parts, recall the dreamer to the locality. Slumber, deep and refreshing, comes at length, and from the couch of hemlock twigs the sleeper rises early, more elastic than from a feathery nest, ready for the engagements of the day.

A FORTNIGHT IN THE NORTH WOODS.

August, 1867.

The city toiler who breaks away from the sedentary routine of office duty to become a student of Nature in her wildest aspects, and a participator in the excitements of camp life, strikes a vein of enjoyment and a source of healthful influences. Even the weary and often exhausting efforts, under the burden of a weighty knapsack, in filing through the rough paths of the wilderness, find their abundant compensation in the repose around the camp-fire after the day's toil. In the flashes leaping and curling upward from the burning logs, gilding the leafy canopy of towering trees, through whose network the heavens display their glory, while the far-spreading lake is speaking through myriad wavelets breaking upon the sandy beach, there is an inspiring accompaniment to the stories of former experience with the rod and gun, making the flying hours a prelude to the night's rest upon a bed of hemlock tips.

The route to Fort Edward by the flying locomotive is but the experience of ordinary steam traveling where incident is not expected, and the only concern is to span intervening points in the quickest time. Here the iron horse leaves us for more primitive means of travel, and the stagecoach exhibits the mechanical success of squeezing the largest amount of humanity into the smallest possible compass from which the occupants can be taken out alive. Passing over a sandy flat, the Half-Way House to Lake George uniformly waters the horses and offers additional beverages to those who dislike to give up the custom of traveling by *steam*.

The historic grounds of Warren county have their permanent landmarks in the monument erected to Gen. Williams, and in Bloody Pond adjacent, and carry the observer back to the days of the French and Indian Wars, when human slaughter wore its fiercest aspects, and to conquer or die was less a choice than a necessity. The panorama of dale and mountain, with its far-stretch of cultivated fields and frequent village indentations, catches the admiring eye from an elevation soon after leaving Glens Falls, forming one of the finest views on the route to North Woods. After a ten-mile ride, as the road leads down the summit, the far-stretch of Lake George is a picture of rare beauty. Soon we reach the county seat of Warren, an attractive summer resort to those who can exchange brick-walled marts of trade during the heated term for the avenues of lake and forest, the earnest of the wilderness stretching far beyond. The village of Warrensburg is a jewel in this rough setting, and its neatness and quiet beauty arrest the traveler's eye, suggesting the fancy that it may have been dropped ready-made into a picturesque locality. Here are several elegant buildings which would be noted for their finish and surroundings in more pretentious settlements. An extensive tannery is a profitable business resource of the place. While tarrying here for dinner, one of our party had occasion to examine his traveling bag, but the discovery made and the comments elicited cannot touch the reader as it did the interested party grouped around the remains of what had been once fair to the eye. It was more regretful to the loser, from the fact that it had been presented to him by a thoughtful parishioner to meet the need of a possible contingency in the exposures and dangers of wilderness life. In the reminiscences of after years, we have no doubt the little band there assembled will be with the scene in all its primal freshness and spirit, though far sundered in the flesh.

From Warrensburg to Johnsburg is another staging of about the same distance: but the heavy globe-like stage-coach is here exchanged for the lesser demands of travel, and a two-horse wagon takes the mail and such comers as may need transportation. In the summer season passengers are mainly of the class like our party, bound for the woods. The scenery now takes on a rougher aspect, the mountains looming up still grander, often with seamed and scarred fronts, as if the ages were stamping their wearing work upon them.

Soon after leaving Warrensburg the Hudson river rolls in sight, and the road runs for many miles on its banks, often cut upon the precipitous sides of a mountain, where the earth above wears a threatening look of a slide, and the descent is so sheer that the traveler is reminded of the midway perils of Scilla and Charybdis. About half way between the two villages is " The Glen," an embryo settlement consisting of three modest tenements, one of which is a " watering " place. Here the route crosses the Hudson by a spacious and high covered bridge, and the river, though still comparatively narrow, begins to take on some of the larger proportions of its after grandeur of sweep. If any loosening and friction of the joints and muscles were necessary for an introduction to the discipline of the woods, it is most effectually accomplished by the staging up and down on this part of the journey.

Johnsburg can hardly be called a place of growing importance, the only noticeable addition, during the seven years the writer has annually supped there, being an elegant house

recently erected by Mr. Robert Waddle, who is the leading
business man of the place. The public house is kept by his
brother, who is totally blind. Yet he moves about the
premises as though the full light of day flashed within and
greets the arriving visitors whom he has met before with a
hearty welcome by name, guided to the recognition solely
by the sound of their voice. He converses freely like one
cognizant of passing events, apparently seeing as much
through the eyes of others as they do themselves.

One more (and the last) staging is from Johnsburg to North
River, about twelve miles distant, following the bank of the
river. This is a settlement made up of about thirty houses,
a small house of worship with no regular service, owing to
the sparseness of population, two hotels, and a store. The
public houses find profitable custom from summer hunting
parties who take this, the usual route into the southern camping grounds of the Adirondacks, and from their guides, who
on their return take the earliest opportunity to transfer their
liberal wages into the hotel cash-box, and wait for another
chance to recruit. The residents find occupation at tilling
the soil during the summer months, but lumbering is the
main dependence. As soon as the demands of the soil have
ceased, labor seeks the lumber regions which commence, and
finds good remuneration in felling the pine, spruce and
hemlock. The logs are drawn to the borders of the nearest
water-course, which in winter, when the heavy snows make a
broad highway, is a comparatively easy task, and when the
spring freshets come they are sent on their downward destination to Glens Falls. To secure their passage, which is often
interrupted by becoming wedged together forming a "jam,"
men known as "river drivers" are employed at $5 per
day, to follow the floating treasure and keep it in motion.
The occupation is full of peril, the drivers often being compelled to force their way among the wedged logs, through the
turbulent waters, needing a quick eye and active limbs to avoid
danger. With the utmost caution they occasionally fall victims in the treacherous contest. The lumbering is carried on

by companies, each of whom has an ownership mark which is registered in the State Archives at Albany. This brand is stamped on the butt of each log owned by a company, and the defacing or imitating of which is an offense severely punishable.

On leaving North River we take our last look at the outside world and apparel for the woods. And here is a proper place to introduce my companions, whom I shall designate as George, Hyatt and John. George is one of the pioneer hunters of the North Woods. He is one of a trio, with Chauncey and Crit, who have carried their hunting and fishing implements over a large portion of the mountain ranges of the Adirondacks, and kindled their camp-fires on the borders of its numerous lakes. In the pursuit of deer their " jack " lights have flashed by night into every bend of lake and river, familiar visitants, and their successful guns waked the echoes far and wide through the mountain passes of this region. George takes to a hunter's life as one to the manner born — fertile in resources, strong in endurance, and skillful in execution. Hyatt was the philosopher and humorist of the party, ready for any emergency, with willing hand and cheerful word. John was on his experimental trip to the North Woods, yet was destined to win his diploma for whatever he turned his hand to, and his constructive skill was of good account.

Our luggage, or that portion of it deemed essential for the camp — always over-estimated in quantity — was placed on a heavy wagon drawn by two stalwart horses. Our day's destination was to Dick Jackson's, at Cedar river, a distance of fourteen miles. It was too much like work at the opening to be called a pleasure tramp. It frequently was a diversion, besides enlarging our stock of scientific knowledge, to sit down at short ranges on the verdant banks, and deliberate on the botanic specimens which grew so luxuriant around us. We never could see the philosophy in such a situation of traveling as if escaping from fire, pestilence and famine, and were scant of time to accomplish the job. This hint may explain why two of the party on the tramp sat down semi-occasionally to examine the state of their heels.

3

Griffin's clearing is one of the landmarks of this region, a place for the accommodation of man and beast. There we paused with five miles of our destination yet before us. At this point we caught sight of the towering peak of Blue mountain, looming in the far distance above all other peaks, and at whose base lay the queen of lakes, where our camp altars were to be erected. The sight put new life into us.

Our route lay over the Indian river, which we soon reached. Standing upon the bridge which spanned it, as far as the eye could reach on either side was one dense mass of logs packed so close as to entirely shut the water from view. These logs were not sufficiently advanced to take advantage of last spring's freshet, and now waited the next moving of the waters.

We passed Hoxie's Variety Store at Indian river, where hunters are supplied with the requisite articles for their occupation. It is also a post-office delivery by courtesy, and the mails are carried out and brought in once a week by a boy on horseback. Hoxie is one of the originals of the North Woods, and a sketch of his hunting career would be an interesting narrative. But we must leave that to others more conversant with his versatile career in that wild region.

Jackson's fine clearing in the valley of the Cedar river is in view, and we know from experience there is all the weary traveler can ask in store for us. As a housekeeper, Mrs. Jackson is appreciated by all who have sat down to the table prepared by her, and it is made a double relish by her pleasant welcome. Richard Jackson's clearing comprises over three hundred acres in the river valley, and a finer farm is not often seen, if the luxuriance of its crops is any basis of judgment. Grass, oats, rye, barley, buckwheat, potatoes and ruta bagas, all were in a condition which told the successful hand of labor and the strength of the soil. Last year he harvested one thousand two hundred bushels of oats — this year about one thousand was the estimate. It may be asked where is the market for such crops at this out-of-the-way place? We answer that the winter's demand of the lumbering interest takes all he can spare, at prices much higher than our Dutchess farmers ever realize.

A good night's rest — the last between sheets we were to have for many nights — with a bountiful morning's repast, prepared us for the outward forest stretch. Our luggage was again taken in charge by Mr. Jackson's team and driver, and we took to the woods beyond his clearing, with eight miles between us and Rock river. We had procured a boat of Jackson and forwarded it by the wagon. Reaching Rock river we landed our boat and shipped our cargo, but had struck our oars only a few times, when we espied Chauncey approaching in a boat. We were to be tenants of his cabin grounds at Blue Mountain lake, and the meeting at this point was in accordance with previous arrangements.

We have alluded to the newcomer as one of the trio of well-known hunters in the North Woods. Chauncey Hathron is entitled to something more than a passing notice in this narrative. Seven years ago he was engaged in mercantile business in Saratoga. Failing health induced him to spend a few weeks in the North Woods, and the restoring influences of the change were so manifest that he gave up his business and made his home in these solitudes. Of late years his comfortable cabin is on the border of Blue Mountain lake, where, with his two dogs as his constant companions, he traverses in all seasons the dense forests in every direction, launching his boats and casting his lines in the cluster of waters, and gathering venison and trout for Lake George, Saratoga, and other summer resorts. "Old Trim," his eldest canine companion, is known and admired far and near through these forest haunts as a model of his breed, and his sonorous bay is a pretty sure indication that his swift and unerring feet are tracking the flying deer to its water refuge. Trim captured his first deer with the aid of our companion George, and hence always welcomes his revisits to his forest home with especial recognition. The tourist in the Adirondacks is fortunate in securing the *chaperonage* of Chauncey and his canine companions. If the deer and trout are at such times within the reach of hunter or angler

skill, he can count safely upon an exciting and successful
season.

But to return from our digression, to the launching of our
boat on Rock river, where Chauncey took us in charge. This
is a sinuous and rapid stream, in many places deep, where the
fallen trees prong out thickly, making the rower's task still
more twisting, if possible, than the line of the crooked waters.
It is an accretion from the springs which flow bounteously
from the mountains adjacent, and its prevailing icy tempera-
ture makes it one of the finest trout streams of the region.
Its marshy banks are also favorite feeding places for deer.
The noble large stuffed buck's head, ornamenting the walls
of Kuhn's International Restaurant in our city, was captured
by George a few years since upon this river.

After a six miles row we struck the landing from which a
path across the base of the mountain leads to Chauncey's
cabin, about a mile distant; leaving George and Chauncey at
the cabin to rehearse old times, the rest of us chose to begin
camp life in a comfortable bark shanty a few rods distant on
the beach, whose white, even and hard-beaten sand was a welcome change from the wild and rough tramp of the inner
forest.

This magnificent expanse of water is put down on some
maps as Lake Emmons. But we prefer to call it by the more
familiar name in hunter vocabulary, of Blue Mountain — its
godfather, around whose lofty summit white mists linger and
clouds dally, looking down in sentinel duty over it. Of the
numerous water basins, stretching out to the vision from the
summit of the mountain, there is none to surpass, few to compare with this lake, in the grandeur of its surroundings or its
surface beauty. Twenty-two islands, some of them acres in
extent and covered with evergreens, intersect the view and
add their ever-varying charms.

The closing of the shades of night was a signal of repose.
Chauncey had fallen a hemlock and its tips were gathered for
our mattress use. Spreading our rubber blankets over them,
with knapsacks for pillows and a blanket covering, we locked

out upon the blazing logs just beyond the safety line, and watched the curling flames shooting up as if to reach the lights of heaven, which gleamed down through the fluttering leaves, whose rustling music was another impalpable key "striking the electric chain wherewith we are darkly bound." But all the poetry of the scene, and the slumber which belonged more essentially to the hour, were ruthlessly dashed by Hyatt's inexhaustible drolleries, who seemed determined to celebrate our advent to camp life with lively demonstrations of regard. What with "poking up the fire" by adding rapid combustibles, until we began to fear for the safety of our shanty, and poking up our risibles by equally sparkling jokes, the light and laughter shook out from the domain of silence all its darkness and gravity, and bluffed off for a time even the screech owls, who had commenced their solemn voices of the night.

Morning came, and with it the necessity for a breakfast. At the entrance upon camp life this need is but moderately pressing, but each day brings its increase of appetite, until the approach of a repast is regarded with absorbing interest, and rations are consumed, which to the often coy and dainty appetite of city life would have been regarded as an awful punishment. Our table was independent of carving and polish — very simple in form and structural detail. The nearest approach to varnish was what had been left upon it by the insufficient action of the dishcloth. Seats were improvised which answered all the purposes of the best upholstered article. A cooking stove was transferred from Chauncey's cabin, and tin cups and plates, knives and forks of different and antique patterns, with other minor appendages of primitive housekeeping, constituted a sufficient setting out for a camp, proving that there is one condition at least where it is true that "man wants but little here below."

I am not going into the details of our pantry and cooking, further than to say, that hung upon trees adjacent were some fine specimens of native meat, and that trout were ready in abundance for the stove before their flecked raiment had lost

its gold and purple lustre. And if any doubt exists as to
Chauncey's ability to make such supplies palatable, we inter-
pose the voucher, that the table rarely had enough left upon
it " for manners," or the dogs. But we cannot leave our
table department, sanctified to memory by Hyatt's regular
appeal to " fry the pork crisp," without replying, at least so
far as *our* camp was concerned, to a lady correspondent of the
New York *Sunday Times*, who thus discourses :—

"Those amateur sportsmen who camp out for weeks every
summer would resent any imputations upon their neatness;
but oh, what pots and pans and gridirons have been seen in
the improvised pot-closet in a tent up in the woods! What
dishes! what knives! what towels whereupon they wipe
every thing from a goblet to a fish! They call it primitive
housekeeping — and that it is! Pepper and tobacco lie in
friendly contiguity to the bit of pork that is to give a zest to
the dinner of birds (not herbs). Pipes and bread are not far
apart, and a jack-knife thrust into the butter answers every
purpose. Think of these degenerate Nimrods, so dainty at
home that a speck of dust on a table, or a little roughness of
starch on a shirt collar, is not to be tolerated for a moment!
But put them, as it were, where like Peter, they have only to
'Arise, kill and eat,' and oh! what horrible things they will
do under the general head of 'camping out!' When fish
succeeds fish *they* do not waste time washing dishes, and day
after day the same proprietor claims the same cup and knife
and fork."

This writer must have been relating her experience among
the heathen! We can vouch that our dishes were regularly
washed — although when getting ready for a day's outing, it
must be confessed the dish water was sometimes hurried
through its office. And as to the scandalous allusion to
towels, had the writer witnessed, as we did repeatedly, Hyatt
putting our dish-wiper through a solution of soap and water,
she would have been convinced that there were exceptions to
her censure. Granted that some neophyte in housekeeping
among us, with more zeal than knowledge, may have acci-

dentally used the pot-cloth instead of the dish towel (we *had*
both), yet where is even the best regulated kitchen in which
some mistakes do not occur ?

An afternoon excursion in boats down the lake brought to
view two deers feeding leisurely upon the bank of the lake.
We watched them intently for a long time, then as we
approached they loped into the woods. Six or eight years
ago the deer in this region had been comparatively so little
disturbed that they roamed freely in the day-time, and were
no unusual sight to the hunter. Now it is changed. They
rarely come down to the lake until darkness hides them from
view.

"Watching for deer" is a pastime requiring time, patience
and sharpness of vision. To Hyatt and myself, on one occasion, was assigned a position on an island at the lower end of
the lake. We commenced duty in the most approved manner,
intently straining our eyes in every direction, as vigilant
sentinels, but our patience was unrewarded. Panther mountain rose to the west of us — so named from its being a favorite
retreat of that animal. Our attention was arrested by a
peculiar cry, as from some object moving along the side of
the mountain. · We were ready to vote it was a panther, but
had no desire to make a closer investigation. True, there was
a liberal bounty offered to any one who would bag one of
these troublesome creatures, chip off its ears, and take it to
the proper place for paying the bounty. But we had a trust
assigned us — to watch for deer — and we could not in honor
indulge in the luxury of hunting bear or panther.

The panther, as well as the bear and wolf, are occasionally
killed in the mountains bordering this lake. Chauncey has
killed two panthers in his hunting experience in these woods.
During the winter, wolves are frequently seen, and when
driven by hunger, sometimes loiter on the borders of the lake,
waiting to pick up the dead fish-bait left by the fishermen.
While the snow lies deep the wolves are very destructive to
the deer, the latter being unable to move fast enough through
the snow to escape from their more agile foe. Bears also

abound, and many are trapped in the winter months, their
robes bringing a valuable compensation. A large one was
seen on the road by which we entered, as we were informed
by a party who followed us. The red raspberry bushes grow
large and have a prolific yield wherever a clearing has been
made, and of this fruit the bear is very fond. The idea of
danger from these animals is scouted by guides and other residents, who pass through the wildest part of the woods, day
and night, without fear of interruption by them, and do not
carry arms with any idea of needed protection from danger.
They say that when seen, these wild habitants of the woods
seem anxious only to escape, and no instance is known of their
attacking a person.

Our diligence as watchmen abated, as no sound of hound
or game broke the monotony. Hyatt made the acquaintance
of a stalwart bullfrog, which reciprocated his intention by
working shoreward. He characterized it as a Daniel Webster
of the waters. Its broad forehead, expansive chest, and dignity of expression and deportment were expatiated upon, until the thought struck him that Daniel Webster's hind legs
could be turned to account as an addition to our larder. No
sooner said than done — the great expounder of double-bass
swung in air pendulant from a fish-pole, and others of his fel-
lows whose hinder propellers had wasted their sweetness to no
particular benefit of mankind, were soon added to the booty,
making a collection which would have set a. Frenchman
dancing.

Our companions had all left their watching places and returned gameless to the camp. We heard their recall by the
report of a gun; we struck for the camp, and had reached
within half a mile of it, when Hyatt sung out there was a
deer in the lake. We turned and saw it cleaving the waters
and pressing for the shore. Though much fatigued from the
long row we had just taken around the margin of the lake,
we pushed in the chase and progressed fast enough to turn
it back. As we drew near the expected prize it wheeled and
again plunged shoreward, and outspeeded us in the manœuvre

When in range again Hyatt discharged both barrels of the
gun with excited aim, without other visible effect than to
stimulate the deer to greater speed. We had started with
but two loaded shells, and our ammunition being exhausted
we were left in the condition of the "foolish virgins," lamps
out and oil left in camp, so there was nothing to do but to
row for it. The report of the gun had signaled Chauncey
and George, who put out from the camp to assist in the capture. Our duty was to keep the deer in the lake until reinforcement arrived, and we made a good beginning, holding it
in the lake. But we failed in our tactics by getting abreast
of the game instead of guarding the rear. The deer was
quick to see the opportunity, and with a sudden wheel it
struck with renewed energy for the shore, about three rods
distant, our boat only reaching abreast again too late. As it
rose to the bank the other boat had reached within shot, and
a trigger was pulled, which, had the cap responded, would
doubtless have changed the result; but it didn't — the only
report being a *concussive* report from Chauncey, and as the
flying deer, who had nobly earned his life and liberty, like his
prototype of Scott's creation in the " Lady of the Lake," as —

> "Bounding forward free and far,
> Sought the wild heaths of Uam Var."

the ludicrousness of the scramble became intensely apparent.
A more " blowed " couple than that which panted in our boat
could hardly be imagined. We retired leisurely and gracefully from the contest, musing on the uncertainties which
often dash the most earnest efforts and expectations, and were
willing the subject should be dropped.

On the first lowery day an excursion to the lower lakes between Blue Mountain and Raquette, was decided upon. Our
party, in two boats, set out with the intention of spending
the day at Loon brook, a famous trouting stream. The outlet
of Blue Mountain lake is a narrow chasm, thickly studded
with surface rocks. A half a mile of this channel, under
overhanging branches and between projecting boulders,

brought us into Eagles' Nest, a lake of picturesque setting, so named by E. C. Judson, better known by his *nom de plume* of " Ned Buntline."

On the southern bank of Eagles' Nest, on a clearing of about forty acres, Ned erected a neat tenement, with the covering novelty for this region of shingles and clap-boards. Here for years he buried himself from the outer world, and wrote his sensational stories for newspapers and magazines. A short distance from the house there is an oblong verdant plot, bordered with evergreens, where lie the remains of his youthful wife, who shared with him the loneliness and privations of his wilderness home. The sacred associations which cluster around every grave appealed with peculiar force from this secluded mound, as yet rarely visited by human foot. No memorial stone or inscription is here, and the sepulchral rites must of necessity have been in accordance with the lonely scene. Yet the towering trees are ever sighing through their foliage, and from the swelling lake which washes its sloping bank, comes an almost ceaseless sympathizing utterance in fitting requiem of one whose life was thus isolated, and who sleeps so far from her kindred.

Ned's cabin is now occupied by a laborer, Mr. Harrington, in the employ of the company who owns this township, and we were indebted to him and his wife for the baking process by which our camp was supplied with good bread.

Passing down the lake we espied among the tops of a dry tree an eagle's nest, which indorsed the appropriateness of the name Ned had given to the lake. We soon reached Loon brook, which enters from the north about midway of the lake. The indications of a wet day had now become apparent. The rain, the first we had experienced since entering the woods, now fell in occasional dashes, suited to the business on which we were soon actively engaged. John, " the beloved," soon demonstrated that he was a fisherman in another than his usual field, and his successes were only interrupted by exclamations of satisfaction as the finny beauties rolled over in the boat from his line. The trout rose slow and sluggish to the fly, but the bait dropped down into their cold deep nooks, got the better of their coyness, and our success was ample, several of the trout running into their second poundage.

The near proximity of the sun to the mountain tops warned us that our lines must be wound up, and our boat was turned again down the lake. A few moments' rowing brought us to the connecting passage with another lake. Lake Utawana, as Buntline christened one of the prettiest links of this chain upon which we now entered, has many points of attraction. But the gathering shades of night and the increasing rainfall were not favorable to rhapsody, and however indifferent to a soak the angler may be, while he has a busy rod as a non-conductor in his hand, he is inclined to meditate in a different mood when his thoughts are left alone with the emptying clouds. At the foot of the lake which had given us a two miles' row, we struck the landing leading to one of Chauncey's bark shanties, on the bank of the outlet of Marion river, which is the main inlet of Raquette lake, about eight miles distant. Our shanty, though leaking and cramped in size, afforded a welcome retreat ; and here, huddled in camp companionship, with a fire of logs blazing at our feet, we rehearsed the incidents of the day, smoked the calumet of peace, and dried our saturated garments. The situation, could it have been seen at that juncture, might have excited unnecessary sympathy in certain quarters. Exercise, appetite, and pure air fortify the system against apparently adverse elements, and make of no material account what, under different circumstances, would be regarded as grave disturbances. There is many an unstrung invalid whose quickest antidote, if not only adequate remedy, can be found in just such discipline and practice under Nature's healing code.

As our venison was exhausted, and there was no ingenious Rebekah, as of old, to " prepare savory meat from the flock," we resolved that the next best thing was to propose that Chauncey and George should take a night-hunt on Marion river for deer. As the crop of mosquitoes on the river was unusually fertile this season, it was no pleasant task to sit

like a statue in a boat, hour after hour, while the silent paddler sent its bow into every nook and branching sweep of its
waters where the deer would be likely to feed. But there
was no flinching. Our purveyors left us to the quiet of the
camp-fire, while the still unbroken clouds, though temporarily
withholding their contents, gloomed darkly over us. It was
in the gray of the morning when our hunters returned with a
fine buck, another deer having been captured and left behind,
as overtaxing the capacity of the boat, but which was soon
added to our stores.

Marion river is a noted resort of the hunter and angler.
Like Rock river it is serpentine in its course, and in its deep
holes there is ample sport with the rod. As we have already
stated, this river, formed of the outflow of the three-mentioned
lakes, runs some eight miles into the Raquette, and boating
is good the entire distance. Our first intention was to pass
through the Raquette into the Fulton chain beyond. But
the indications of continuous wet weather, and the limit of
our time nearly reached, we reluctantly abandoned the pro-
ject. Two days in our narrow shanty, with constant scudding
clouds that frequently play their liquid anthem on the tree-
tops, made us desire our first quarters at Blue Mountain, and
before night we packed up and were on the back stretch.
The rain finished its mission for the time in a grand thunder-
storm, than which, with such surroundings, nothing could be
more impressive. The loud peals were caught up and prolonged by the echoes, which are here repeated with surprising
distinctness. Just before the storm, Chauncey and George
started for Eagles' Nest for a supply of bread, and had not
progressed far before it burst upon them. They could only
mark their position by the frequently recurring lightning
flashes, and one tremendous peal was so near that it shook the
oars out of their hands. They felt their way through the narrow passages, and before they reached camp were under a
clear sky.

The last evening of our camp sojourn had arrived. Strong
as were the inducements beckoning us out of the woods, there

was a feeling akin to regret that the sun was setting upon the last day of our sport in the Adirondacks. We pushed our boat from the shore, three of us as occupants and George in another, leaving them to their own drifting motion by wind and wave when we had struck deep water, and gazed upon the glories of an evening sky, the beauties of whose cloud tints no pen or pencil can portray. We watched its changes through all shadings, crimson, rose, violet, and gold, upon a deep blue ground. The mountains rolled backward and upward from the lake, peak over peak, until upon the farthest in view the sun was disappearing. Meanwhile Hyatt and John discoursed of sunset scenes in their traveling observations in the old world, agreeing that this, at least, was an exception to the poet's contrast.

> "Slow sinks, more lovely ere his race be run,
> Along Morea's hills the setting sun —
> Not, as in Northern climes, obscurely bright,
> But one unclouded blaze of living light."

And what were George's meditations as he floated, in reclining posture, the smoke-wreaths of his pipe, like fancy's airy creations, seen but a moment and then vanishing. We thought we could read them wandering back to earlier wood life, when Chain lakes heard his rifle first, among those who sought the seclusion of these romantic hunting grounds, and now weaving anew the web of incident, woven of many colored experiences. Perchance musing over the unsparing work of the woodman's axe, thinning forests and damming streams, by which the deer and trout had been driven from their long accustomed haunts. For there are changes, even here, where an unaccustomed observer would suppose change could hardly ever come ; and year after year plodders for money are making noticeable inroads upon the old forests, which must send the seeker farther and farther back in pursuit of game.

But the sun painting has faded from the sky, and visions of the past, evoked under such influences to move with their charm before us, must also yield to the sobering realities ever in their train. In the early light of morning we were on the return carry, and bade adieu to Old Blue mountain.

4

LOWER SARANAC AND RAQUETTE LAKES.

No. I.

July 30, 1869.

I write you from the head of Long lake, where Palmer, well known to all visitors of the northern wilderness, keeps open house and dispenses generous hospitality.

My visit to this region finds me in company with an experienced associate in camp life, for the first time on the northern route of entrance. It has the advantage of novelty of scenery, and a long stretch of boating by lake and river, more attractive in many respects than the continuous jolting of stage travel. But it has far less seclusions of pursuit than is found on the North river route. Those who entertain strangers say there has never been such a rush of visitors. Blood at the Saranac, Bartlett at Round lake, Johnson at the Rapids of Raquette river, and Palmer, our present host, have all been at their wits' end to know where to dispose of those who have sought their quarters, and many have found it difficult to get a meal or a night's shelter. The exaggerated descriptions which have been published of sport in the Adirondacks have drawn hundreds to this section, who have found it was not all their fancy painted it. If they ever come again it will be under sobered and wiser calculations for such a trip.

On the afternoon of the third day from home we reached Bartlett's, a very pleasant stopping place between Round and Upper Saranac lake. About midnight, while the rain was pouring profusely, a party called for accommodations who had just come in from below. They reported the loss of one of their guides, by the name of Ed. Curtis. It appeared he was intoxicated, and, while endeavoring to manage his bark canoe, lurched overboard. His companions heard his cry and went back, but found only his empty canoe and floating hat. This is the second guide who has found a whisky grave in the lakes in this section within a short time.

On leaving Bartlett's we took the first lesson in shouldering knapsacks. The carry to Lower Saranac, however, was but a short half mile, and didn't try muscle very severely. At Johnson's carry, at the Rapids of the Raquette, there was a mile and a half to surmount, much of the way a steep upgrade. If my knapsack, which a close calculation would have put at about fifty pounds, didn't reach one hundred and fifty before I got through that slippery up track, then I was under a great delusion.

The hunters are complaining more earnestly than ever, of the scarcity of deer. I learn that Murray, the "bookmaker" of the Adirondacks, has killed only one so far, although he has been here for some time with a large company.

By the way, they tell a good story of the great fisherman and hunter — on paper — to some incredulous reader of his great exploit, which is illustrated by the tip of his pole crossing its butt with two trout pendulous. In order to show the sceptics how it could be done, Murray stepped into a boat, pole in one hand, placed his foot on one side of the bow, leaning upon which too heavily caused the stern to sheer suddenly in the opposite direction, and over went the Adirondack historian, *kersplash* into the water. His listeners saw the point of his illustration.

To-day we start for Raquette lake, and whither from thence, circumstances must determine.

No. II.

RAQUETTE LAKE, *August* 5.

In my last brief note I informed you of our arrival at Palmer's, at Long lake. At noon on the day following, having procured a boat of Palmer, and necessary camp supplies, such as pork, potatoes, flour, butter, etc., we started for this point. We found at Long lake an old guide acquaintance, whom we induced to accompany us part of the way.

Passing from the head of Long lake we struck Raquette river again, and followed it to the Rapids, known as Buttermilk Falls, where Murray locates his adventure of the Indian maid Phantom, and the imaginary descent of his boat, with himself and guide over the abyss. These Falls are worth seeing. The river for several rods dashes over the thickly studded rocks, which churn the swift current into a foaming avalanche down, down into a wide and tranquil bed. No boat could ride these waters in safety.

At the foot of the Falls we enter upon the carry of a mile and a half which leads to Forked lake. Here our guide left us, as we had struck familiar waters. This lake is about four miles long. At its head we reached the third and last carry, between Long lake and Raquette, about half a mile long, and here George essayed his first attempt in boat carrying. Our craft weighed plump one hundred and ten pounds, and was no trifling lift. After some little delay, in which the question of success hung in doubt, it rose upon the shoulders of struggling humanity a monument of pluck and perseverance, and with conquering steps it was soon launched upon the far famed lake, which has since been our stopping place. Turning south, we passed the Raquette House, on the left, kept by Carey, a well-known resort to the North Woods hunters. Soon after we passed an island known as Indian Point, for many years the home of Mrs. Beach, one of the two pioneers of this section. It is now temporarily occupied by Tait, a New York artist of high repute as a game painter, and one of the most skillful sportsmen in these waters. Just above, on the right, is the Wood place, built and for many years kept by "old Wood," whose history runs back to the first public attention directed to this grand sheet of inland water. Here we found George's old friend, Sid. Hayes, who has been its occupant for several years. He received us with warm hospitality and made us feel at home. As I had rowed some ten miles during the afternoon, for the first time within the year handling an oar, the offer was peculiarly appreciated. No fatigue, however, could make one insensible to the rare beauty of scenery which spreads out on all sides from the elevated positions. Lakes, islands and mountains meet the eye on every side, and, from their varying points of beauty, never tire the vision.

Sid. Hayes, the present occupant of the Wood place, was formerly a bank-note artist in New York, in which business

he was a skillful workman. The change in the character of our currency, which threw out of existence our State banks, broke up to a great extent the occupation of those engaged in this business, and Hayes was attracted to this locality, as a lover of its beautiful scenery, and one having a keen relish for its exciting sports. He is a frank, true-hearted gentleman of cultivated tastes, and universally esteemed among his acquaintances.

While I am writing, Hayes has just returned with some fifteen or twenty pounds of trout, caught in the lake, some of them over a pound in weight. It is an indication of the peculiarity of the season, that, at this lateness of the summer period, brook trout should be mostly found in the deep waters of the lake, instead of the spring-holes of the streams. They are very scarce at the latter places. The weather continues quite cold, with prevailing north winds and frequent rain.

The camp of Mr. Murray and his party is on an island, nearly opposite Hayes' residence. An evening or two since we were on a rise of ground near the head of the east inlet, "smudging" off the flies and mosquitos, which are very abundant this season, and waiting for the shades of evening to set in for a "float" down the river. A party of boats came down with ladies and gentlemen, and one boat stopping at our landing, a man in hunter's garb came up to our fire bringing a teapot, and asked the privilege of sharing it with us. In the conversation which followed, we learned that our visitor, Mr. Murray, was tarrying on the same business as ourselves. Having partaken of his frugal meal, and enlivened the same with pleasant stories of wood life, it was arranged that he should have the first chance down. Not long after, loud snorting, or, as it is called, "whistling," was heard, showing that one deer had taken the alarm in time to save himself from a pretty sure shot. We followed soon after and were served with the same music from two other deer. They were feeding on the marsh adjoining the stream, which furnishes feed so fresh that there was no sufficient attraction in the grass and lily buds in the water's edge.

The hunters complain of the scarcity of deer this summer. The extreme coldness of the season may account for this, keeping them back in the shelter of the woods.

In a day or two we propose a brief visit to our old camping ground at Blue Mountain.

III.

OUTWARD BOUND, *August* 19.

Post-carriers out of the woods are few and far between. Hence, if the convenience for writing should offer, the prospect is that any temporary visitor to these parts will be likely to reach home as quick as his letters.

Since my last we have serpentined through lakes, and up and down the cold water brooks leading into them, and caught fish-bites and mosquito-bites in about equal proportion.

The fly-rod of the latter is a wonderful contrivance, and the victim is very apt to " rise " when it is thrown. You touch a bush with your passing boat, and out go a swarm of these river songsters, following you as if their first and only chance for blood depended upon putting you through. There is no use in trying to outstrip them. I have watched with interested curiosity their speed, and am satisfied that in a three mile quick pull they will come out the freshest at the end, " nip and tuck " with you.

Contractors for game at the lakes have raised their prices, and are now paying sixty cents a pound for brook trout, about forty cents for lake trout, and twenty cents for venison. Of course, the contractors who sell at Lake George, Saratoga, and other summer resorts realize a still higher return. These prices give to those who make angling and hunting a business very lucrative wages, but the curse of whisky, and the poorest kind at that, consumes the whole, with the greater part of this class.

Parties are coming and going at the Raquette this season more numerously than ever. Few of them are prepared to accept the annoyances and hardships of such an excursion, for the real solid good which can be derived from it. But it is equally true that in the same old ruts of daily occupation, both mind and body become shortened in their powers, and so contracted within narrow orbits as to lose sense of enjoyment intended for daily use. The excitements here with the rod and gun, and the discomforts of the insect world, levying tribute or collecting revenue, are but incidentals to the great end of sharpening the eye from glorious far-off looks, or quickening the ear in the lighted boat on the midnight paddle, listening for the footfall of the red deer. If you miss your deer or trout you are still the winner. Your needed training is going on. Like the smoker's meerschaum, you not only "color" beautifully, but feel that it is the sign and seal of recuperating forces within, while your quickened lungs beat their silent tune with a new sense of pleasant existence. You can get spunky when any thing goes unsatisfactory, just as quickly here as anywhere else, but then you have the advantage that you can get over it quicker, for the ridiculousness of getting out of patience amid such surroundings is sublimely apparent. And then for a lodge in the wilderness improvised from hasty materials, and, before rolling in your blankets for the night, to watch, with an appealing appetite as I have, George broiling a trout or slice of pork on a crotched twig, and pulling his moustaches the meanwhile, as if there were some invisible sympathy between them and the simmering coffee over the coals; and we have given glimpses of life in the woods which the lover of Nature in her freedom and wildness will hold as a lingering charm.

Among the visitors to the Raquette we have had the pleasure of meeting Mr. J. H. Mathews, who is recreating here for a few days, accompanied by a friend from New York. They enter with zest into the occupations of wood life, and will doubtless reap its benefits.

We also had a call from Mitchell Sabattis, the clever and experienced guide, who accompanied Messrs. Lossing and Buckingham on their explorations of the sources of the Hudson and to the top of Mount Marcy, a few years ago. He inquired about them with much apparent interest.

Chilly, cloudy weather has been the rule rather than the exception, so far during this season. On the night of August 8th a frost that would have done credit to December wilted and browned corn to the roots in some places. When we reached Dick Jackson's clearing we found him busily engaged in haying. He calculates on one hundred tons this season, a pretty good cut for a mountain farmer, fourteen miles from any settlement. Oats are looking very fine in this region, with their heavy heads and large stalks. But they hold their greenness still, and frosts are feared. This will be remembered as a cold season among the Adirondacks.

Bears are still seen occasionally on the borders near the clearings. The men whom we passed informed us on our return, that they started one out of the path we had just left. Bruin was wallowing, hog like, in a puddle, but was in such a hurry to leave that he did not stop to shake himself. Such incidents create no sensation among the natives, as the timidity and shyness of bruin are a long established fact among them.

The completion of the Adirondack railroad to Thurman, thirty-eight miles from Saratoga, and within three miles of Warrensburg, makes this by all odds the choice of routes into the North Woods. It is already graded some distance beyond Warrensburg, and will follow the west bank of the Hudson, most of the way along the line of the old abandoned grade commenced several years since.

There is some talk of its being finished to Johnsburg, ten miles from Warrensburg, but this will not be done probably until next season. From thence the rich lumber and iron ore of the forest, not many miles distant, will be reached, and its wheels bear out to the busy world vast treasures now locked in fastnesses where the foot of man is rarely if ever heard. The day that witnesses such an innovation will date the vanishing of much which gives a peculiar attraction to these solitudes; but it will open to common and easy travel, with well-provided accommodations, a magnificence of scenery and purity of atmosphere, far exceeding that of the most favored resorts of the present day.

FROM LOWVILLE TO PLATTSBURGH.

August 5, 1871.

After about a week's absence from my post, it occurs to me that I may make up a brief memoranda of its experiences, etc., and improve an opportunity, somewhat unusual to camp life here, of sending a message out. Leaning against a stump, with my knees for a writing desk, is the choice of position afforded, but the inconvenience of stump writing may save you from the infliction of a long letter.

Mr. Slee and myself reached Lowville Tuesday noon, the day following our departure from P., where we met by appointment a team sent for us by Mr. Charles Fenton, proprietor of well-known quarters to all parties visiting the northern wilderness of this State by this route. Fenton resides at Township No. 4, about eighteen miles from Lowville, over as rough a road for the most of the way as any that has come within my experience of wood travel.

At Fenton's we met the guide he had engaged for us — Danforth Knowlton. Danforth is a Massachusetts-Yankee, a strong-limbed, clever, ingenious specimen of his class. We found him a trusty, willing, and competent guide, and can commend him to all who need the services of such a companion in the North Woods. Seven years ago his desire to follow a hunter's life led him to this section, where he has since followed the occupation of a guide in summer, and a trapper of fur animals in the fall and winter.

Parties from this point uniformly strike for Smith's lake, which is the largest on this route until you reach Big Tupper lake. As there were two or three shanties already occupied on that lake we concluded to defer our visit to that water and turn into Salmon lake, one of the " Red Horse Chain," as it is called.

From Fenton's to Beaver Brook, about eleven miles of rough road, our baggage is carried by a team. We reach Wardwell's House. " Wild Woods Home," after four hours' travel, where a good dinner is provided, and is sure to meet a good appetite.

Our boats are here started on this brook for a run of ten miles up stream. It abounds in deep holes where the trout at this season find their feeding grounds. We took sufficient for our table supply without stopping, and reached the shanty on its bank in time for an early supper and preparation for our first night's lodging in the woods, with our rubber blankets the only separation between us and mother earth. Here we met a veteran dominie with two lads, who had been camping out for ten days, ready to depart on the morrow. They had exhausted their stock of provisions, but, the dominie said, had saved an enormous appetite, and must have something to eat for breakfast, or starve. Our larder was ample and we had the satisfaction of saving them from that calamity.

In the morning we turned northward, boating across Burnt lake, one of the smaller collections of water dignified by that appellation, and reached a carry of a mile and a half. Here came one of the tugs of forest travel. Loads are apportioned somewhat according to capacity on an English racecourse. Yet after footing half a mile or so it would be difficult to convince one of the weaker parties, that he had not been reckoned, in the distribution of the burden, as one of the stallions of the first carrying force.

There is an end to all mortal experiences, and the truth is never accepted with heartier conviction than when water destination breaks upon the sight, to close this pack-horse work. We reach Salmon lake, the second in the Red Horse chain, where we were to pitch our tent. Tired as we were, and thus more acceptably inclined to favorable judgment, we must confess to some disappointment, especially in view of its imposing name. It is a secluded basin about a mile in length, and from a third to half a mile in width, with few points jutting out to break the straightness of line, and not an islet on its bosom. The view is shut in entirely by gentle eminences, unrelieved by a single commanding peak. We struck it near the outlet, and while our guide went back for the balance of our supplies, sat and watched the rising of a heavy cloud, of threatening aspect. The first pattering drops

warned us to seek shelter, and spreading our rubber blankets
over our traps, and turning our boat over, we crawled beneath
its cover, and enjoyed in security an outpouring of rain. Our
guide returned as the clouds were breaking up, and soon we
were paddling for the upper end of the lake, selected for our
headquarters. With a tent well bedded with hemlock boughs,
and a blazing camp-fire before it, the roughest place in the
wilderness is soon transformed into a scene of comparative
comfort. The cold, rainy weather, which set in steadily for
two or three days, found us well sheltered, and we could
listen to the roaring of the thunder and the music of the
winds among the swaying branches of the overhanging trees,
with an added sense of the grandeur of Nature, in her tempest phases.

But there are also lessons of instruction in humbler aspects.
Looking out of the tent opening in the morning, we beheld
our guide, in shirt and vest only, sitting on a log, mending
his pantaloons, defiant of the keen morning air. He explained
the severe simplicity of his attire, by saying that he had forgotten to bring an extra pair with him, and thus allayed apprehensions of his sanity. It was a suggestive hint of the importance of being doubly provided against the wear and tear of
wood travel, as one never realizes more fully under such circumstances " what a day may bring forth "— and require covering.

Salmon lake may have been better entitled to this name in
bygone days. At present the salmon (or lake trout) are not frequent captures. Only one of this kind has as yet displayed
his proportions in our boat. But with speckled trout it
abounds in good measure, and we have taken all we need —
some of fine size. While engaged in this sport on the second
evening, a deer came down to the bank, in handy distance for
a rifle, but the prohibitory statute protection had not quite
expired, and what may have been more prohibitory, our rifle
was in camp. The animal parted from view, with an admoni-
tory whistle to his kind that an enemy had arrived.

The delusion must be given up that these beautiful tenants
of the great northern wilderness, which once were seen

throughout the day disporting in the waters, have now any portion of it left to themselves, where they can be thus visible. Bullet and buckshot have largely done the work of extermination, and now they must be sought with many disappointments, and are rarely seen. Even in this locality, where no party has left encampment evidences preceding us for many months, presence of deer is only traceable by their occasional footprints in nightly visitation to the streams running in and out.

But if the deer are diminishing, the insect world still hold their own, and are ready to die game at all hours. The deer-fly, the mosquito, the midge or punkie, are fresh and fearless as ever. Some one has said, "Man's love is of himself a thing apart." It is not so of the love of the insect biting world for him. There is no "apart" ideas of relation in their philosophy. "Thine forever," or as the Yankee phrased it more appropriately, "Yours tu death," seems to be their being's end and aim. We have speculated whether the expansion of the muscles of the arms, which occurs during a sojourn in the woods, is not owing mainly to the rapidity, strength and frequency of motion in brushing away these disturbances. Of the three kinds named, as "sample bricks," the least in size and biggest in consequence is the punkie. The mosquito announces his coming with a grand flourish of his trumpet. The deer-fly leaves no sting of any account behind. But the punkie, if you see it at all, is only a little black speck, which you marvel is sufficient for organism of life, yet he bites ferociously, crawls up into your hair and down your neck, and raises a blotch on some victims like a mosquito. It swarms in early morning and at evening, and is prolific on water-courses. Passing up the inlet of the lake with the guide, the other evening, we watched him brushing away these pests, until his quiet speech took the utterance of " d——n the punkies !" With both hands lively engaged in like occupation, we felt that there was an inclination of responsive weakness on our part, even under most guarded duty of expression.

The other three lakes of this chain are Witch Hopple, Nigger and Crooked. We made an excursion to the first named, to try a night float for deer. Its name, we are told, comes from an interlacing stout vinelike bush which grows in rank abundance and "hopples" your progress. The distance is about fifteen minutes' walk. It is a beautiful little lake, of lesser size than Salmon, but with a much finer setting and surroundings. We made our way to a winter log shanty which our guide had built for his trapping uses, back from the lake among the heavy timber. It was arranged that Slee and the guide should go out on the lake for a night hunt, and like Robinson Crusoe I was left for the time monarch of all I surveyed.

We can conceive of no fuller sense of solitude than the isolation of trapper life in this spot. Some forty-four miles away from any village settlement, and a great portion of that distance away from any human habitation, it must be more an infatuation for the wild and stirring pursuit of the occupation than the chances of profit, that draws him hither. Looking out upon the hoary old trees, lighted by the flickering blaze of the camp-fire, where the axe of commerce has not yet felled a tree, and the forest has only yielded its tribute to the needful uses of the hunter, his is the teaching of the vastness and antiquity of the earth, of which civilized life has only a dwarfed and faint conception. And yet what changes must have followed successively even here, since the native owners and occupants wooed their dusky beauties to their wigwams, and took their spoils in easy abundance from forest and lake. The panther, bear, and wolf, the common prey of his bow and knife, have also largely disappeared, and the deer and trout must soon be comparatively among the things that were, if they have not nearly reached that state.

One feature, however, remains, upon which the changing influence of time has fallen slightly. These beautiful lakes, with their clear, cold waters sparkling in sunlight, or waved by the storm, still remain in many places untouched by the hand of utility, seemingly as perfect in their charm as when the primal light burst upon them.

5

The night hunters return, and report no sound or sight of
deer, and once more we gather to our blankets and lowly
couch.

Our return route is laid out up the remainder of Stillwater
to Albany and Smith lakes, through the Tupper and Saranacs
to Plattsburgh to Lake Champlain homeward.

No. II.

My previous letter left us in a state of preparation for a
movement farther into the wilderness. Camp life explains
the propensity of settlers on the frontier to break up their
quarters on a sudden impulse, and give their clearing axe a
more solitary sound beyond its wonted field of labor. The
eye longs for new surprises, and imagination pictures more
stirring scenes. This is no difficult process where the home
shelter is so readily constructed, and some new El Dorado
looms up invitingly in the distance.

A half an hour's labor enables us to take up our tent, pack
our supplies, and walk. Returning on the trail we had entered, we launched our boat again on Beaver river, and turned
up the stream for Albany lake, our destination for the night.
This river, from Stillwater, where we first struck it, to Albany
lake, has a run of about twenty-five miles, much of the way
with a rapid current. Its turnings and windings can be understood from the fact that it is only about nine miles by land,
through the forest that lines its banks. The work of the oar
in making the passage is greatly increased by the effort required to keep the boat on a turn with the stream, and the
constant lookout ahead to dodge partially submerged rocks.
Dinner hour overtook us in willing humor, as it inevitably
will under such circumstances, and we landed at an inviting
place on the bank of the river. Getting dinner in the woods
is a simple process. After kindling a fire, the next invariable
requisites are a crotch and pole. These two articles are
staple commodities in camp life. To make your temporary
shanty for a night's lodging, or prepare your dinner, crotches
and poles do wonders.

The guide had driven a crotched stick just back of the fire, and pushed a sharpened pole obliquely in the ground, leaving a short projection resting on the crotch over the fire, from which the coffee pot was soon to send out its steaming odor, when he informed one of the party that there was a famous spring-hole not far distant in the forest, where large trout could be taken.

Fisherman took the bait at once and started through the dense mass of alders, in the direction pointed out. After floundering about a half an hour among the vine-twisted underbrush, now picking up his hat, then releasing his tackle from a fettering twig or vine, he came out again in astonishment near the place he had entered, to behold his companions quietly dispatching dinner. Whether it was a ruse on the part of the guide to get the start at dinner, or a pious fraud to give the angler a better relish for it, by preliminary exercise, is an unsolved riddle; but of one thing he is certain, that the locality of that spring-hole, and the cause of his coming out at the same hole he entered, are a mystery, although he found about every thing else, in his flounderings through bushy labyrinths.

"Time and tide wait for none," and we had one of these, and an equivalent in the rapid current for the other, to contend with. The sun was dropping low toward a mountain top, as we resumed our progress, with a carry ahead, and Albany lake yet at working distance. After about an hour's row we struck the rapids, where for about a mile the river dashes downward through a bed of rocks, giving wild music to wilder scenery. Here with knapsacks, blankets, hunting and fishing implements, and other camp equipage, back weighted and hands full, we took the narrow trail through the woods, leaving the guide to drag his boat between and over the rocks which line the passage. Coming out ahead at boating water, we waited for him, and seated on a rock out in the stream watched the new section of the world to us through the curling smoke of a cigar. Presently Danforth hove in sight, tugging and lifting his swinging craft, which seemed to be as obstinate of propulsion as the Irishman's pig, " which frisked about so he couldn't count him." Guide evidently had seen trouble. The rapids were emphatically denounced, and the loss of paint and other damage to his boat, by its frisky collision with the rocks, and the amount of labor he had experienced, were duly descanted. We gently reminded him of the favorite air which, with genuine Yankee drawl, he was wont to enliven every occupation--

"Never sit down with a tear or a frown,
But paddle your own canoe,"

but the jest was evidently too practical, and in moody silence we gathered again to the home stretch and night quarters, thinking of the ideas of a jolly time and no drawbacks, which some who have an itch for camp life in the wilderness entertain.

Albany lake is a charming stretch of water, abounding with lake and brook trout, and a favorite resort of deer. Its lower extremity spreads out into a beautiful bay, which affords attractive grounds for the rod and line. Passing this, its waters again contract, leaving close quarters for a boat through the lilies and rushes which spread over its surface. At the head of this marshy passage are some large stones, the foundation remains of a bridge connecting an old State military road, which many years ago was opened through this section. When it was made, or for what special purpose used for military transportation, we could not learn. The road is overgrown and almost obliterated, but that doubtful quantity, a hunter's story, says it can be followed in its entire length through the northern wilderness.

The lower portion of the main valley of the lake soon came in view, but a long sweeping curve still shut off the bulk of waters extending above it. We chose for our encampment an elevated point, and in a few moments our tent was in position, bed gathered from neighboring hemlocks, and supper in preparation. Our camp-fire glanced far off upon the still surface of the lake, and "the loon's lone cry" at intervals

broke the silence. With the first novelty of the situation worn off, sleep deep and refreshing after a day of hard exercise held us firmly until morning. There is an almost magical restorative effect from such a couch, where the pure air of the mountains can get freely at the lungs. It requires contrivance at first to adjust yourself to an occasional inequality of some projecting twig, but practice makes perfect, and it soon comes round all right. I may remark in passing, as I was informed by Mr. Blood, of Lower Saranac hotel, that a party from Utica left his place for a short stay at Big Tupper lake, among whom was an invalid lady. After a month's trial of camping experience she wrote back to him that she concluded to stay six weeks longer, was able to eat fried pork with the heartiest of them, and to share untired in their wood rambles.

It is expected in camp life in this region that venison and trout will be usual dishes on the table. But sometimes from necessity, if not choice, the bill of fare is varied. Our bill of fare during a day's sojourn on this lake was hasty pudding and maple sugar for breakfast, a wild-duck stew with dumplings for dinner, and frogs' hind-quarters for supper. If any doubt the adaptedness and relish of such entertainment to the situation, let them try it and learn how easy it is to be mistaken. True, my companion eyed the dumplings with suspicion, and thought they were rather "hefty," but it was only a momentary weakness, a lingering tribute to home fashions, as nothing was left to show the skill of the cook but satisfied appetite.

Early in the morning following we were again on the move, and passing the bend in the lake, had a splendid view by early sunlight of the upper and finest portion of the lake. Its entire length is about four miles, and from a half to three-quarters of a mile in width, and it is surrounded by an unbroken wilderness. At the time we visited it there was no other party on it. We learned that parties who had preceded us had been very successful in capturing deer, several of these animals having been seen in the day-time feeding upon its banks.

Near the upper end of the lake, on the left, we struck the trail for Smith's lake, which is a carry of three-quarters of a mile. The crossing is well defined, and comparatively easy, as the bulk of the travel through this section is to this lake, which is a favorite resort for several parties, who have for years made it their summer encampment.

No. III.

Smith's lake, at which place my last note of wilderness travel left us, bounds the summit level of water. It is the last collection in this line of basins which flow southerly as a tributary through the Mohawk and Hudson to the Atlantic. " Charley Pond," as it is called, the nearest water to it on the north, falls in the opposite direction northerly to the St. Lawrence.

This lake is the largest we have met so far on this route, and has many points of beauty. In its general contour it has much resemblance to Blue Mountain lake, and in size nearly equals it. A Syracuse party, some half dozen in number, had just left as we entered it. Another party from Philadelphia had recently completed a month's encampment on its banks, and both were quite successful with the rod and gun.

Smith's lake, at least so says hunter's legend, takes its name from a misanthrope by that name, who some thirty years ago fled from society and made his hermit home here, on account of domestic troubles. The foundations of his log house are still visible, and a once extensive clearing made by him, for the uses of fuel and other purposes, is now covered with hardwood trees, which uniformly succeed the original pine, hemlock, etc. Passing through the old clearing, fifteen minutes' climb of the mountain brings to view a splendid panorama of lake and wilderness stretches, presenting a vivid sectional survey of the vast amount of timber resources, not yet reached by railroad or continuous water transportation.

Two sons of Mr. Wesson, the inventor of firearms, bearing his name, with two youthful companions, all of them in their "teens," with three guides, were in camp here, highly enjoying the situation, and full of marvelous experiences. We captured the only deer of our roving trip on the outlet of this lake, after a long night hunt reaching into the morning hours.

On the morning of the third day following our entrance upon it, we were again aboard, steering for the upper end of the lake. Here a very passable carry of a mile and a half brought us to Charley Pond, whose waters, as we have stated, are the turning point in a northerly direction. With the exception of three or four hours during midday the air was sharp and frosty, and woolen blankets and a substantial camp-fire were comfortable additions to our night's lodgings.

About a mile down the pond is the carry of half a mile to Little Tupper, which has an inlet from this source of about three miles, easy and pleasant boating. We stopped on the way at spring-holes pointed out by the guide and had a fine catch of trout. Our camp was pitched on a prominence running out in the lake, covered by yellow pines, the first timber of this kind we had noticed. While enjoying our evening meal a boat came up the lake, in which were a gentleman and lady, and approached our quarters. They inquired if we had seen a guide who had started out in the morning with his dog to drive in a deer. At that moment a loud call was heard from some distance on the opposite shore, and they put off to meet him. Other boats containing ladies were seen gliding over the lake during the evening. The presence of dry goods, even in the bloomer costume, was novel and refreshing, and my companion and the guide began to pay a little more attention to their toilet.

Little Tupper is the usual boundary in these Nature's wayside travels from a northerly direction. And indeed there is no need of going further to find expanse of water, attractive seclusion and wildness of scenery. Of irregular surface, dotted by islands, and spreading out into capacious bays, it affords all desirable employment for rod and rifle, in the best season of such sport. From its main inlet to the outlet it reaches about seven miles, and its geographical surroundings must for years to come defy the incursion of lumbermen.

At break of day our craft was pointing down the lake. The fog was so thick we could not see a boat's length ahead. Occasionally the dusky outline of trees required us to solve whether we were approaching shore or an island. The sun finally got sufficient mastery of the fog, to point the way, and show we had not wandered much from the desired direction. There were two camps, on an extensive scale, occupied at this the finest portion of the lake, one of them including several ladies.

The outlet of Little Tupper is through a marsh of water plants, covering the surface so completely that a little way off no passage can be seen for boating. We threaded our way many acres through the lilies, and entered a round lake about two miles long. At its foot a series of picturesque rapids commence, and for a mile or so the water boils over obstructions into deep basins, which catch the eye as choice place for trout, in the season when they lie at the rifts. On the carry along these rapids we met with several shanties, which doubtless had been occupied by successful sportsmen during May and June. Stillwater now favored us until we reached the dam and saw-mill at the head of Big Tupper lake, the first evidence of the creative hand of civilization we had seen for weeks. It is but a few steps, and our boat and baggage are let down an embankment into these last-mentioned waters.

No. IV.

Big Tupper is a greater favorite with pilgrims to the North Woods than its little namesake, perhaps because it requires less physical exertion to reach it. Their titles, however, are calculated to deceive an inquirer, as in size there is hardly sufficient difference to warrant the distinction. At some distant day, when the voice of the iron horse shall echo through the mountain gorges surrounding them, they will doubtless be identified by more imposing titles.

At various points on the main shore, as well as on the islands, white tents glistened in the fading sunlight, indicating the more numerous proximity of fellow mortals once more. Boats filled with both sexes were moving upon the waters, and mingling song and merry laughter came upon the ear in pleasant contrast with the surroundings.

There are two well-known houses for the accommodation of visitors on this lake. Graves, a Boston man, at the upper end, has nearly completed a spacious edifice, well-finished and painted, which in addition to his old quarters will enable him to furnish ample room for the increasing summer travel to this locality. At the lower end, Moodie's place, in a beautiful pine grove, commanding a fine view of the lake, is well patronized. Moodie is an old hunter and boatman, homely and pleasant in his ways, and does his best to make his guests comfortable. Here we met our young townsman, Charley Cornwall, who has been boarding with Moody since last spring, and is captivated with attractions of this out-of-the-way life. A few days previous he met with a very lively incident in undertaking a feat which is not laid down as of any practical value in hunter's tactics. While out in a boat alone on the lake, he encountered a buck, and went for him. He grappled the animal's tail, but not expediting matters fast enough by that hitch, he changed his hold to the other end, and essayed to pull him in by the horns. This suited buck, and his forefeet immediately stuck over the side of the boat, to assist in the operation, dipping in a large cargo of water. The copartnership was suddenly dissolved, and this novel process for capturing a deer in water was postponed to a more convenient season. Charley privately informed us that he meant to try to bag a bear the coming winter. Should he encounter bruin there will be no lack of pluck and resources on the part of the young hunter. Should he be compelled to run he is developing a surprising length of legs, which would give him a decided advantage in the race.

We looked back upon Big Tupper with a lingering desire for a longer acquaintance, as we shot out of its waters in the

morning. Raquette river comes down with a sweeping
curve almost to its bank, and receiving its waters through a
very short outlet, bears them northwardly to the St. Lawrence.
Our route lay up the Raquette to the right, a charming row
of some twelve miles. We passed several parties going in.
In one boat, containing an oarsman and lady, there was a domestic history, whose particulars we did not learn until we
reached the Lower Saranac, where the parties resided. There
we were informed that the man was a guide eloping with a
married woman, bound for love in a shanty somewhere in the
woods. She had left a family of six children, the oldest but
twelve years. Perhaps the most defensible view of Shake-
speare's

> "Frailty, thy name is woman,"

is furnished when there are six abandoned young children to
back up the sentiment. As for the husband in this case, the
trial was not considered so serious that it could not be as-
suaged by a well-filled whisky bottle, and neither party were
quoted as models of domestic virtue. The neighbors did not
seem to regard the affair as any " great shakes," but if one of
our Poughkeepsie reporters had been there to work it up and
interview the parties, what a magnificent sensation could have
been gotten up over a desolated hearthstone and blighted
domestic happiness.

We reached Daniel's (formerly Sweeney's) carry, and found
the old gentleman with his horse and cart ready to take our
boat and baggage. The carry is three miles long, over a very
good road, which has been worked at considerable expense
through the forest. Two dollars and fifty cents, his charge
for transportation, is very reasonable. Daniels is a veteran,
verging on threescore and ten, and talked glibly of his experience as a soldier for the Union in the recent Civil war. He was
at the battle of Fredericksburg, and in active service until the
close of the war. At that battle he was prostrated by a dis-
mounted gun knocked over by a rebel shot, and somewhat
injured, but with this exception escaped harmless. His son

resides at the Upper Saranac end of the carry, and during the travel months they find busy and lucrative employment.

Crossing the Upper Saranac to Bartlett's carry, which is but a few moments' work, our luggage is again transferred by team to Saranac river, which we pass down, through Round lake and Three Mile river into Lower Saranac, the last of boat travel. About eight miles row and we are at Martin's, where we part with the services of our guide, and soon reach Blood's Hotel. Having stopped there before, we were prepared to find good quarters and excellent accommodations. His teams are ready for service to bring parties out, and those who desire it can take the Wilmington Pass Route, through the notch in the mountains, passing John Brown's old homestead and the place where he lies buried. This ride, for the unsurpassed sublimity of its scenery, is alone worth a trip to this place.

Dropping down again to the routine of wonted tasks, the recollection of scenes and incidents, refreshing to body and mind, and sweetening accompanying toil, is doubtless in their recapitulation more interesting to the writer than to the reader.

IN CANADA WATERS.

RAPIDS DES JOACHIM, CANADA WEST, ?
July 22, 1872.   ?

We left Sand Point on the steamer *Prince Arthur*, bound up the lake to Gould's Landing, about twenty miles distant. It was a snug, swift and powerful boat, built for the rough work in which it makes daily trips, extending some fifteen or twenty miles above our landing. Much of the way she had to encounter rafts of logs, now being hurried down with extra force, to reach the market before the summer heat lowers the streams above. One immense raft of logs covered the surface of the lake, and detained us nearly an hour. Scores of single logs, escaped from the boom within which they had been chained at the start, were floating on the lake, and over these the steamer plowed its way, a successful case of steamboat corduroy travel. Frequently the pilot's slowing bell warned the engineer that one of these obstructions was in the course of the boat. There was a crowd of lumbermen on board, who had been out of the bush for a spree, and had evidently brought a large portion of it back with them.

These lumbermen constitute mainly the population of this portion of Canada. Two-thirds of them are of Indian descent, the largest part of them pure blood. They are hired for a term of sixty days, ninety days, or a year, and generally are faithful in service, while in the bush, where no whisky can be got. They fell the pine, the only lumber here sought, a good portion of which is hewed to the square before it is committed to float. The logs are sent down singly, but the hewed lumber is spiked together in what are called "cribs," two layers of massive logs, one crossing the other, and usually committed to the charge of two men, who guide them down the Ottawa river, and over the rapids which give name to this place, to the level and broad expanse of the same river below the long stretch of boiling and whirling water, which forms an impetuous disturbance of this stream of rare interest to the beholder. But to the mode of lumber transit over the rapids I may allude again.

It will thus be seen that these rough, if not scarcely half-civilized men, have a life which requires great muscular activity and powers of endurance to meet its daily demands, and that once out of its routine, where they are fed by hard tack and pork as staple supplies, it is perhaps natural, if not wise, that they fly to the extreme of indulgence, and make up when released in uproarious dissipation for perforced abstinence.

But to return to our steamer. Escaped from the booms and floating logs we had a pleasant run, including a novel experience of a steamboat ride through a considerable stretch of rapids, in the upper part of the lake, where an island divides the waters, leaving a narrow channel of falling waters as the only passage.

Reaching Gould's Landing we were transferred in two-horse wagons, several of which were ready to receive the large number of passengers, returning to the bush, as forest life is here called. Our land carriage extended about fifteen miles to Muskrat lake. I may have seen a rougher road, but I do not now remember where, unless it was a subsequent stretch of land travel of about the same distance that night, which connected the steamboat route with Pembroke.

At Mud lake another steamer, a miniature craft, was in waiting, fired up. What with passengers, luggage and freight, it was a novel spectacle at this remove from any thing which looked like ordinary channels of business intercourse. And yet, as opportunity subsequently convinced us, this wild thoroughfare is one of vast extent and immense profit to the commercial association which mainly monopolizes it. It is called the Union Forwarding Company, who transport through this line by land and water connections, reaching beyond this place some twenty miles, and now building boats for further interior points, all the supplies for the settlements and lumbermen encampments. Sawed lumber for building materials, dry goods of all descriptions, clothing, provisions and forage are delivered here over this route in quantities that surprise one new to its demands and resources. Included in this traffic are all the supplies required for the southern wants of the vast fur gathering business of the Hudson Bay Company, which has at this place its lower post.

The trip up Muskrat lake by moonlight was charming. Without change of position we pass into Mud lake, which is simply a narrowing of this sheet of water, of shoaler capacity. Why these good enough names of the aboriginal lords of these waters should not now give place to prettier titles is a natural inquiry. But romance is at a large discount here, and things will run in their old rut till the change sure to all localities shall come.

We reached Pembroke about midnight, an old-fashioned place, where the simple tenements built in less active business days, before lumbering became so important a staple give

6

aspect to the surroundings. The next morning the little steamer *Pembroke* took us aboard up the Ottawa river for Des Joachim, which we reached soon after meridian, and found comfortable quarters at McDougal's Hotel, a very quiet, well-conducted house, where every attention is paid to guests.

Here we met with our correspondent, Mr. Spence, agent at this post for the Hudson Bay Company. It is due to acknowledge our indebtedness to him for many favors and courtesies freely rendered, and of much advantage to us. Indeed, throughout our entire Canadian trip we found hospitality and kindly aid on steamer and land, the more agreeable as it was not sought on our part, or paraded on the part of the givers.

We found splendid pike and pickerel fishing in the bay formed by a turn in the Ottawa just below the rapids; and in a small lake, about two miles from this place, we took an abundance of black bass, some of heavy size.

We were somewhat disappointed on reaching this place to learn that two Indian guides, who had been engaged for us, had been tempted into the lumbering service, by the high wages which are now paid, and the scarcity of laborers needed to close up the rafting business of the season, now becoming impeded by the falling of the river. Although about six hundred miles from home, we had intended about another hundred miles' travel into the wilderness, above marts of traffic, in order to reach a more abundant game region. But under these circumstances we are compelled to halt here, and take our chances. We have engaged a couple of Indians long enough to carry our camp equipage and canoe to Trout lake, about five miles distant, and start to-morrow, where I may possibly recount experiences. Till then, adieu.

No. II.

TROUT LAKE, *July* 28.

A dull, drizzling day, with a cold easterly wind, which strikes our smouldering fire and drives the smoke directly into camp, where we are reclining on our rubber blankets. Is there any thing more contrary than smoke? You stand by a

camp-fire and it comes puffing up into your face; you shift position, and by some mysterious law of attraction it faces you again without delay. As I turn over the pages of a work of fiction, which George considerately put into his knapsack for such a contingency of weather, my tears would delight the author as an evidence of power of his pathos. Not willing to admit that the smoke — which we have endured so long together, by many a camp-fire, kindled by the side of almost every lake in the North Woods — can so overcome us, George suggests it is a tearful outgushing of homesickness. This conclusion I resist with the argument, that this disturbance in genuine form attacks but once, and thereby vaccinates against recurrence.

Across the portage from Des Joachim, about two miles, over a good road, the communication by steamboat is again resumed, and extends up the Ottawa some twelve or fifteen miles.

Before leaving Des Joachim — (this settlement name is a capital one to practise upon, and the variety of its utterances would amuse the Frenchman who first invented it; the most accepted one is *De Swish-ah*) — before leaving it, I was about to say, we went up to the head of the rapids to witness the employment of the raftsmen. As I stated in my last, the greater portion of the timber is sent down singly in logs of uniform length, and after passing the rapids it is gathered and confined by an outer series of logs, chained at either end in a continuous circuit. But there is another class of hewed lumber, composed of sticks twenty feet or more in length, fifteen to eighteen inches square, clear and straight, which are pinned together in a double layer, called "cribs." About a dozen logs in each layer make up these cribs. A dam is constructed across the river above the rapids, having an outlet in the shape of a flume, but a little wider than a crib, and running some distance down to the edge of the boiling waters. The two raftsmen upon a crib start their unwieldy craft by the aid of strips of plank for oars, playing between two pins on the outside timber, and pass slowly toward the flume, or "slide," as it is called. No sooner does it reach this inclined flume, than it shoots with great velocity into the whirlpool, and while you look with expectation for a general burst-up, and the raftsmen overboard, their steady, practised eye and hand have kept their craft in a direct course, down like an arrow's flight through a quarter of a mile of bulging and roaring rapids on every side. Sometimes, with the utmost care, but more likely through negligence of duty at the critical moment, the crib swerves from the direct course, and striking a sunken rock flies into disorder, and the raftsmen spring into the water to escape collision with the wreck. Two lives were lost this spring at the slide above from this cause.

These slides, which are found on all the many streams leading from the vast timber districts of this country, are constructed and owned by the Provincial government. Our landlord at Des Joachim holds the office of slide-master from the government, and his duty is to keep account of every crib which passed safely through. Each crib pays a duty of two dollars. The last raft which was formed below the rapids this season was composed of one hundred and twenty-two cribs, which gives some idea of the profit to the government from this source.

But this is not the only source of revenue from the timber trade. The forests are disposed of at auction, in divisions called "limits," covering a territory of fifty to one hundred miles, and the price for choice limits sometimes runs up to seventy or eighty thousand dollars. This does not include the land the right of which the government retains, and settlers may enter at any time on a limit and occupy such portion as they may desire for farming purposes. This is not unfrequently the case, as there is a large demand for forage for lumbermen's teams, and oats and hay can be raised in good growth — the former selling at present for $1.00 a bushel, and the latter not unfrequently in demand at as high a price as $50 and $60 a ton.

We started for Trout lake under the guidance of two Indians, whom we were able to coax away from hayfield en-

gagements by an extra remuneration, aided by drizzling and
unsuitable weather for field work. And such a burden as
they will shoulder is a marvel. A large pack, weighted with
provisions, cooking utensils, ammunition and the many
et ceteras for camp life, is secured by a long portage strap,
made for the purpose, leaving the portion of it in the
center, where it has the width of about two inches, to pass
over the head and rest against the forehead, the only
hold the pack has upon them. Upon this they piled the
tent, knapsacks and other loose materials, and then lifted a
canoe upon their heads, and bending to the load started up
the mountain path, leaving us with our light equipment quick
work to keep up. A stretch of five miles through a blind
path, matted with underbrush, up one side of a mountain and
down the other, promised sharp exercise to city legs. A sense
of the strangeness of the situation and dependence upon our
leaders kept us for the first part of the tramp in close file.
But becoming more accustomed to the tramp, and more self-
reliant, we loitered to notice peculiarities of the surroundings.
Our self-confidence, however, was sadly misplaced. Hurrying
up to regain our guides we found ourselves alone, on one of the
blindest portions of the route, with scarcely a sign of a trodden path. For three-quarters of an hour we floundered in the
brush, and only by accident we stumbled upon a direction at
last which brought us to the place where they were sitting on
a fallen tree, and apparently waiting for us to turn up. We
expected at least a lively war whoop of satisfaction at our good
fortune in finding ourselves again in the right way. But
without a word of inquiry or expression of concern, they resumed the march, as if their business extended solely to the
care of the baggage, and not of its owners.

Talking of Indians, I am reminded of an incident told us,
suggestive of days in this country when they were not so
harmless neighbors as at present. About twenty years ago, a
family by the name of BUTLER constructed a rude home on
the Ottawa river, opposite Pembroke. Soon afterward their
youngest child, a boy of three years, suddenly disappeared,

and traces of him were sought in vain. They suspected he had been stolen by the Indians, and diligent inquiry was made among all the settlements of that race, even as high up as Des Joachim, which was then only a post of the Hudson Bay Company, for traffic with the natives. But years passed in hopeless research, and at last they gave up inquiry, and dreamed no more of his return. Last spring some one who had heard of their loss, mentioned that he had seen a young man at a settlement not many miles distant, who had such a history attached to him. The father immediately started to investigate the case, and found a youth now twenty years of age, whom he believed to be his long missed son. The only recollections the latter had of his childhood were that he lived with the Indians until about seven years of age, when they sold him to a French half-breed, who used him harshly, and he finally ran away. On their return, the mother, keener in parental perception, recognized distinctive marks upon his person, which the lapse of time had been equally powerless to efface from her memory.

The case of another family in the same vicinity was mentioned, who suffered a like loss, through the same agency. Possessed of considerable means, they spent it all and impoverished themselves, in vain efforts far and near to regain their lost one. But no tidings of him have been heard.

On reaching Trout lake the dusk of evening was thickening upon us. Our guides soon pitched the tent, gathered its bed of hemlock branch tips, and roused a cheering fire. Weariness had settled into every muscle and joint, as we squatted and watched our dusky companions fill a large frying pan with substantial slices of salt pork. But our stomachs were not ready for so dainty a repast. If, however, we had entertained any doubts that it was good, they certainly were not shared by our help. They cleaned the pan of the solids and sopped up the remainder with their bread, and in the fullness of their quiet and unemotional enjoyment it would have been a severe stretch of fancy to find application for "Lo, the poor Indian." The idea occurred, that for Lo's appetite one might be reconciled to be Indian, at least during a meal time.

When we "tucked in" that night, it was in accordance with the most loyal devotion to the regulations of Congress — without distinction of race, color, or nativity. Side by side of a stalwart red-skin six footer I lay — the past all forgotten and forgiven. I bore him no grudge because some of his far-off ancestors might have made havoc with the capillary covering of a pilgrim forefather, or have danced around a blazing circuit of fire to which they may have consigned him. I had no apprehensions for my own scalp; I knew that to lift much hair there would puzzle even savage ingenuity. But there was a novelty in the situation not congenial to ready slumber, and it was natural that I took advantage of the light thrown from the camp-fire to turn a side glance at his bronzed features. But I saw nothing except the perfect picture of repose — such as a couple of pounds of fried pork, and a lining of whisky (for the Indian rarely parts with that) might be supposed to give. If he did not sleep the sleep of the just, it was none of my business, at that late hour. The sighing of the winds through the pine tops whose motion we could see overhead, and the murmur of the waters of the lake close to our feet, brought sleep defiant of novel bedfellows and a hemlock mattress with twigs as big as your little finger, and very impressive on your first introduction to such a couch.

As mentioned in my introduction, a rainy day confines us to camp, and gives opportunity for these rough pencil sketchings.

Trout lake is a small basin of water, about a mile and a half in length and three-quarters broad. It does not compare in beauty of surroundings with hundreds of like mountain reservoirs in the North Woods of our State. Indeed I have seen nothing of Canada scenery as yet that bears such comparison. There is a lack in contrast of altitude of mountain and magnitude and denseness of timber growth. Farther in the wilds of this country it may be that this difference is less apparent. The Matteawan and Des Moines rivers, above us, I am informed pass through vast heavy timbered territory, and lead to the great lakes of Nepissing and Temishtemang, regions where

Indian and half-breed hunters find profitable occupation during the fall and winter season in trapping for the Hudson Bay Company.   One thing we have ascertained — that the red deer and caribou, the latter slightly different from the former, are few and far between in this portion of the northern forests.   Their range is below us some fifty or sixty miles.   The moose deer, as the large and more solitary species of this race are called, hold possession of the Upper Canada forests, and there seems to be a natural repulsion existing between them. The vast ramifications of the lumber trade, fostered and directly aided as it is by the Canadian goverument, is a constant disturbance of the larger game, and even the moose is rarely seen.

Our lake stopping-place is appropriately named.   Trout can be readily taken in all reasonable abundance, within sight of camp.   Our catch ranged from a quarter of a pound to a pound and a half.   There are much larger ones in its waters, but July is a portion of the year when they rarely come from deep waters to sport with your hook.   Aside from this there is little excitement to daily movements.   The only animal footprints on its shores which are noticeable are the fresh tracks of bears, but these we have no desire to follow up.   Our only companion on the lake is a loon, who is considerably demoralized at our interloping upon his quarters, as he rises occasionally, wings his way over and around our camp, and then settles back to cousider the situation.   At night we hear his lone cry, the very voice of solitude, through the intervals, sounding almost human in its utterance.

And, by the way, George tells in privacy a very good experience in this line, which I must let out.   Some two decades ago, on his first visit to the Adirondacks with a companion, both but lads, they heard on the first night, after they had retired to their log shanty, a strange wild cry out in the depths of the darkness, which they supposed to be some lost fellow-being shouting for help.   They arose and went a piece into the forest, fired their guns and shouted, but the only response was the same weird, mournful cry, coming from different points, as the great northern diver changed its quarters. The startling thought then seized them that the forest was haunted, and they hastened back to camp and barricaded its rude door and watched in fitful apprehension till daylight brought its relief. The next day, while boating on the lake, their feathered ghost gave them a daylight strain of its music, and turned a fund of experience in the hobgoblin line into a capacious joke.

No. III.

My last was dated from Trout lake, which has ceased to be attractive, from its diminutive limits and general quiet. The capture of trout, exciting as the sport may be for a time, becomes a monotonous and indifferent employment after a season of success, especially when you have a camp supply. Our guides had agreed to return at a specified time and take out our camp equipments. As we were ready in advance for a change, we filled our knapsacks with what articles we wanted to carry out, packed the rest in the smallest compass and covered them with a canoe, and shouldering our load with gun in hand took the return path. Our preparations had delayed us until nearly noon of one of the hottest days of the season. The odor of the pine and other forest trees seemed to add to the sultriness of the atmosphere, and weighed as we were we went through a sweating of the first magnitude. The whirr of the partridge was frequently heard, and alighting on trees adjoining our path furnished an easy mark. This game bird is very numerous through this region, and we found no difficulty in changing from fish to a partridge broil. The road seemed to have increased in length and ruggedness, but the difference may be accounted for in the extra burden. There was a sense of great relief as we caught sight of the Ottawa rapids, and the home-like quarters of our friend McDougal on the opposite side of the river.

The next morning we started for McCullom lake, about a mile distant, where by the kindness of Mr. Tait, a canoe had

been sent in and placed at our disposal. We were told that it
abounded in pickerel and black bass, and we found it so.
Our catch was a very fine one, the bass ranging from one to
three pounds, and our largest pickerel a good four pounder.
On taking home our second day's string, a good jag for a dray
cart, we saw by the countenances of the domestics of the
house that they considered the fish market overstocked, and
that we were trespassing on good nature, and we somewhat
reluctantly gave up the business.

An incident occurred on this lake which will do for a fish
story, having the advantage of being as true as it was singular.
One of our trolls was struck, and while being hauled in it encountered an obstruction and parted. This was about ten in
the forenoon. On repassing in the same locality some eight
hours later, Johnny Welsh, our youthful paddler, stopped
the canoe, saying he thought he saw back a little ways a line
wound around the branches of a sunken tree. Going back we
saw sure enough the lost line, tangled among limbs about
eight feet below the surface. The water of this lake is very
clear, and we detected a pickerel captive to the line, and playing around him were several large bass, either from sympathy with his situation, or making sport with his folly.
Johnny gave evidence of ancestral aptitude for wit, by
quietly remarking that they were getting ready to hold a *wake*.
After a half an hour's patient unfolding of the coil with the
paddle reaching down to his arm pit, George brought it up
with a three pound pickerel attached.

This lake is very picturesquely located; most of its stretch is
bordered with lofty rocky cliffs, of sheer descent, and marked in
many places with veins of iron ore. When the lumbering resources fail this country, as in a few years they must, it has
doubtless mineral treasures which will receive profitable attention. To those who enjoy, as we did, a few days' recreation upon its waters with the rod and line, we do not know of a
more attractive and satisfactory resort. With good hotels
near by, at very moderate charges, the river furnishing also
fine sport in the capture of what is known as the "Ottawa

pike," the angler will have no reason to complain of dull employment.

On our return trip we reached the city of Ottawa the second evening after leaving Des Joachim. Instead of stopping at Sand Point we kept the steamer *Prince Arthur* to the lower end of Chats lake, where it connects with a horse railway, of about three miles, the entire distance over trestle work, and said to be the first railway constructed in the Canadas. At the terminus we reach another lake of about thirty miles in this connecting link of travel, where the fine steamer *Jesse-Cassels* was ready to speed us onward. Near the western end of this lake the Ottawa unites with it in a splendid cascade, delighting the eye with its rare beauty. This steamer lands, at its terminus, at Aylmer, quaint and old-fashioned in its general appearance and surroundings, yet withal a very pretty and apparently prosperous village, giving a fine farming outlook. Here we took stage over a good macadamized road to the city of Ottawa, the capital of the Ontario department, where the Canadian Parliament holds its sessions.

We would repeat our expressions of obligation to the captains, clerks and their assistants in charge of the different steamers on the line of the Union Transportation Company in the Western Canada waters. We found them an intelligent, liberal-minded class, taking especial pains to render courtesies and afford information to visitors from the States. While appreciating highly, as well they may, the advantages which they possess in their government policy, and the light burdens which it imposes, they are unreserved in their acknowledgments of obligation to citizens of the States who have entered into business among them, especially in the management of the lumber trade. They assured us that the present prosperity of Canada was owing in a large measure to the superior knowledge in conducting this trade of such citizens from this side as Eddy & Co., Bronson, Weston & Co., Hamilton Brothers, etc. But while benefiting others these firms have struck a mine of wealth for themselves. We were informed that the firm of Eddy & Co. have realized a profit

over all outlays in the lumbering trade this season of over
$200,000. This, with the thousand or more men in their employ,
and the amount of supplies to keep them steadily at work in
the forests, nine months of the year, will afford some idea of
the vastness of this business as conducted by one firm.   And
this explains why, where we expected to find a quiet wilderness, we should hear daily the shrill scream of the incoming
steamer, laden with men and merchandise, hundreds of miles
into the Ottawa wilderness.

My companion having an engagement which called him in
a different direction, I parted with him at Ottawa, after a few
hours' survey of its municipal features.   Taking the rail for
Prescott at 10 P. M., I reached the latter place a little after
midnight.   I was anxious to connect with the morning train
from Ogdensburg to avoid detention over Sunday.   But the
St. Lawrence ferry-boat was laid up for the night.   Runners
for the hotels at Prescott assured me that I could not cross
the river at that hour.   In this state of perplexity a boatman
came up and offered to put me over.   Hotel runners advised
me not to go, said he would fleece me, he was not a safe person, etc.   My desire to cross over led me to accept his offer.
With considerable difficulty, and I thought with somewhat
unsteady steps, he succeeded in getting my heavy trunk into his
rather diminutive boat, and I followed him in, somewhat
dubious that I had made a mistake.   The river at this point
is about a mile and a half in width.   Out into the dark we
moved, and when about half way over my boatman said his
price was three dollars, and he must have his pay, or he
wouldn't go further.   I replied as I had made no terms with
him I shouldn't object to his price, but would pay him nothing until he landed at Ogdensburg, and if that didn't suit
him he might return.   After growling and threatening for
a while, he resumed his oars.   By this time he was pretty
effectually drunk, and beat about in one direction and another, until I was apprehensive of getting more navigation
than the $3 would pay for.   In the meantime he was en-
lightening me on his history.   He had been a printer and

could "wallop the type," as he expressed it, "ahead of any
thing on two legs." Then he took to sailor life on the lakes,
and now he was running a night express between Prescott
and Ogdensburg, and could throw a boat across quicker than
any other man. I observed that he cast frequent glances toward the American shore, and at first supposed he was
watching to see if any of the revenue officials were on the
alert, as our appearance at that hour of the night was sus-
picious enough to attract attention. But we might have
smuggled over half of Canada, for any interference of Uncle
Sam's officials, and just then I should have relished being
overhauled for smuggling. It was another difficulty that
troubled my boatman. He didn't know his bearings any
more than his passenger did. At length we brought up
against a wharf, the top of which was some six feet above us,
and then came an interesting struggle. For a time it was
"nip and tuck," whether the trunk would go up or accompany
my Charon to the bottom. I was in a mood to bet on the latter, and felt as the Irishman did who wagered that his fellow
hodman couldn't carry him on his back up a high ladder;
"when he made one false step I was in hopes I had him."
But drunken perseverance prevailed, and I was landed in the
silence of the night, a quarter of a mile from any hotel. Not
a step further would he budge, as he was in a hurry to get
back and help some other benighted traveler over. As he
stumbled back into his boat, it was a natural suggestion,
whether any sincere mourner would stand over his remains,
as they must, in the order of events, ere long be picked out
of the St. Lawrence.

Finding my way to the Seymour House, where the colored
porter always sleeps with one eye open, I found that a rush
of guests had left but one room unoccupied, and I was assigned to its comfortable quarters. I had accomplished my
purpose, and was compensated for the annoyances, as at the
close of a month's absence, the eye met familiar objects.

7

No. IV.

EAGANSVILLE, RENFREW COUNTY, }
August 3, 1874.   }

We reached Armstrong's, the headquarters of this place, and have been making our arrangements for going into camp on Round lake, about forty miles northwest, following up the Bonne Chere river. This river is the outlet of Round lake, and Golden lake, the former about seven miles long, and the latter about the same dimensions. We strike the river about twenty-five miles above Eagansville, by land conveyance, and from thence by canoes, passing through Golden lake.

These lakes are a popular resort during the fall months. Hunting parties find not only deer in abundance, but also wolves and bears, the latter reported as very numerous this season. Eagansville is a quiet little place, built on both sides of the river, and mainly interested in the lumber trade.

Canada has doubtless an autumnal season of cool and bracing weather, after frost sets in, but in August, beast, bird and fish yield to the sun's sultry influence, and are not at home to anybody who desires their company. This has been peculiarly the case in the present season when a five weeks' drouth lay scorching and shriveling upon land and water.

Northwest of Eagansville, in Renfrew county, are the two lakes above mentioned, big jewels strung on the comparatively slender thread of Bonne Chere river, which running through them finds its outlet in Chats lake, near Sand Point, and is the channel of an immense lumbering trade. The available timber bordering this water-course has been pretty thoroughly cleared out for many miles above the upper lake. Parties purchasing of the Canadian government the right to lumber for a limited term of years have improved their opportunity, until unproductive pine barrens are the unsightly substitute for a once interlacing foliage of towering forests. What the axe has left has been swept by fire, whose tract is a marked feature of this and other wilderness parts of the Dominion where I have traveled.

Round lake, where we camped, abounds in pickerel and lake trout. The former of large size and are caught in abundance. The latter are taken with hook and spear by the Indians by the barrel-full, and laid down by them for winter consumption. Brook trout are rarely found in this lake, as they are not on friendly terms with their bulkier relations of the same family genus. The Madawasca river, which empties into this lake, we were told had a reputation as a trout stream. We followed it one sultry day about three miles to the slides, built for delivering logs over the Falls. A couple of hours fishing here yielded sixteen of good proportions. A second visit was less successful in number, but of larger size. While we were thus engaged, our guide, who had been in the woods shooting wild pigeons, came in and informed us he had seen two bears not far away, and proposed we should make a raid on them, but we did not take impulsively to the offer. It is a sound principle that only one employment can be successfully prosecuted at a time, and of the two we preferred to work a line in the water, even if the fish didn't bite.

And writing of bears we are reminded of a serio-comic incident which occurred during our brief stay at Round lake. A party from Corning, in this State, came in and camped near us. One of their guides, Tom Armstrong, an old woodman familiar with these grounds for a score of years, went out to a beaver meadow early in the afternoon to recover a hatchet he had dropped there. After a long and unsuccessful search he turned to retrace his steps, but had not proceeded far when he heard the growling of a bear, too familiar sound to him to be mistaken in their source, or to excite apprehension. But he was soon made aware that there were a couple of cubs in the programme of exercises, and this put a difficult face on the interview. The cubs trotted before, and Mrs. Bear kept close attention behind, and as Tom was destitute of any weapon of any sort, it was a clear case of discretion being the better part of valor. Up a small tree went Tom, not large enough to allow a side hug of its body to the enraged mother. And here for a moment we leave Tom, with a first-class opportunity to view from his elevated post the lake and its surrounding scenery, and an interesting specimen of the animal kingdom in closer survey.

Our camping ground had increased in population by an accession of two young men from Philadelphia, taking a part of their college vacation in the woods, and of the right material for camp life -- enjoying every thing, and taking to all the little perplexing minutiæ of the situation with exemplary philosophy. Toward night, one after another the boats returned from the fishing grounds on the lake, and supper as usual became a subject of general interest. The din of preparation was soon heard on all sides, and the shades of evening had set in before any note was taken of Tom's prolonged absence. But the inquiry was no sooner started, than surmises were expressed that there was something wrong. To add to the distrust that was creeping over us, one of the party who had remained in the camp during the afternoon, and who was aware of Tom's mission into the woods, recollected that about two hours previous he had heard some one shouting several times, apparently a considerable distance in the woods, but thought it was nothing more than the frolicsome utterance of somebody who wanted to make a noise. This revelation settled all doubt on the mystery. One of our guides, in the vigorous and unrestricted language very noticeable among his class, expressed his solemn belief that Tom had been eaten up by bears, and called for recruits to start at once in search of the victim. A skirmishing party enlisted at once, firing their guns at intervals, and soon a voice of distress came sounding back from the depths of the wilderness. It was Tom's voice sure, still living, but confined and in peril. Firearms were then shouldered by the reserves in camp, dogs were loosed and the rescuing party became formidable. Ever and anon there was a pause in the march, and a signal called for, to obtain the direction.

It was time now for the bear to quake and turn tail. The reinforcement was more than she could encounter, and with a parting growl, giving Tom a full view of her splendid but disappointed set of grinders, she plunged into the thicket with her cubs. The relieving party reached the scene of peril just as Tom, who like Zaccheus had climbed a tree but with less devotional feeling, came down to solid earth again. For three mortal hours he had clung to his slender supports, while bruin had played "the performing bear" with a variety of antics and a savage determination of purpose not visible in the ordinary street performances of her kind. The tree bore scoring marks of her fruitless attempts to reach her prisoner. Tom had begun to despair of rescue, and it looked to him as if she was determined to fight it out on that line. He begged us never to mention to a living soul that he had been treed and held captive for three hours by a bear, as he would never hear the last of it. He had lived over twenty years of varied experience in the woods, but he had never before dodged an issue with a bear.

DOWN THE RAPIDS.

No. I.

August 30, 1873.

In compliance with a friend's request, after a mid-summer's vacation, I will attempt a report of some of the land and water incidents of a new field of adventure, through the waters and forests adjoining the Michagamma and Menominee rivers, the boundary line for a long distance between the States of Michigan and Wisconsin.

By rail to Detroit, from thence directly aboard the staunch and spacious propeller *St. Paul*, and we reached the point where we expected to meet novelty of surroundings. The steward of our vessel, Mr. H. M. Drake, has long been a favorite of the traveling public on this route. His position was no sinecure, for he had to provide "meat in season," as well as other comforts for an army of guests. On the previous trip, the passengers on the *St. Paul*, bound to the different points up the lakes, numbered four hundred and fifty, and there were three hundred and fifty on this passage.

The *St. Paul* slipped her cables about midnight, and running through St. Clair in the darkness, we lost sight of much attractive scenery. Morning brought us in view of Port Huron, a thrifty and pleasant looking town at the foot of Lake Huron. As we looked off from the steamer we thought of the old subscribers to the " *Telegraph*," at that place, with a strong desire to stop and shake hands with them.

" Ten hours going through Huron," said the captain, as we reached the upper end of the lake. Safely and pleasantly our craft glided over it, not always the case in lake navigation ; for the winds often battle fiercely with the steamers. Not many months since a vessel went wildly down into the dark waters of Huron, carrying to a watery grave nearly all on board.

The upper waters of the lake are exceedingly picturesque, dotted with numerous islands, rivaling in romantic scenery the famous "thousand" of the St. Lawrence. At its head, the notable " Sault Ste. Marie," at the foot of St. Mary's river, breaks into rapids for a long distance, compelling access to the waters of Lake Superior by some other channel. To meet this want a canal has been cut through, and we were lifted by two locks to the requisite level. While waiting this process we watched a party of Indians plying their nets in the rapids for white fish, which they were very successful in capturing. While one at the stern steadied a canoe up against the rushing waters, another at the bow thrust a small net down with the current, and we could see the white treasures clearly defined against the darker shade of the meshes which inclosed them.

Darkness overtook us soon after entering Lake Superior, an unwelcome interruption, for the shores are lined with objects of great interest to unfamiliar eyes. We were compelled to turn within for occupation, as a relief from the dull and drear employment of standing by a vessel's railing, on the wide waste of waters, listening to the ceaseless monotone of the clashing waves.

But the little world inside was full of peculiar interest. People of different nationalities and tongues were grouped to-

gether : some doubtless seeking their El Dorado in the mining
and lumbering districts of this inviting section; some, perchance, like ourselves, though in a different direction, courting
recreation and freedom from wonted toils and business cares,
where nature holds her secluded courts with her mountains
and waters; and some, simply "going home," perhaps wondering at the curiosity which could attract others so far.

But there was one class of humanity, several of whom were
on board, standing out sacredly apart in human interest from
all the rest, and yet apparently hopeful, life's last venture involved in the issue. More to these drooping, feeble ones,
gathering their limbs wearily to the burden they bore, were
the health-giving promises of Nature's elixir in this reputed
Bethesda, than all its abundant gold-turning products could
offer to the mere wealth seeker. And one could not avoid the
reflection, how trivial and transitory were all the motives ac-
tuating the rest, compared with the deep yearnings and hopeful anticipations of these fellow mortals, longing for freedom
again from familiar pain and wasting disease.

No. II.

About 9 o'clock Sunday morning the *St. Paul* rounded into
the harbor of Marquette, our destination on Lake Superior.
The port was lined with shipping, mostly employed in the
transportation of iron ore, of which product this place is a
great center. For the delivery of the ore an immense wooden
pier extends some distance into the lake. The loaded ore
cars run on to the pier and drop their contents through slides
or shutes into vessels beneath. Sometimes from thirty to
forty boats are waiting outside for their turn at loading. Cars
are coming and going continuously from the Republic iron
mines — to which we shall have occasion to refer more particularly — and the clatter of dropping ore is familiar music.

The national government has constructed a substantial
breakwater, running out nearly half a mile, for the protection
of shipping. The harbor of Marquette has many points of
rare beauty, of which its citizens may well be proud. It

abounds in good fishing, as a short experience in its waters
amply demonstrated, and it is a popular summer resort.
About every other person has an abiding faith that he may
become the possessor of a valuable mineral deposit, so abundant are the developments of iron, copper and silver in this
region, fine natural specimens of these ores being exhibited
in great variety in business places.

At Marquette we had the pleasure of meeting our friend
and generous assistant in providing the agencies for our
intended excursion — Mr. B. F. CHILDS — previously unknown
to us, except through correspondence. My companion, Mr.
Slee, had played a photographic joke on his brother artist,
having forwarded as his likeness a photograph of Cashier
NORTH, of this city. With this imposing and venerable picture in hand, Mr. CHILDS had perambulated the spacious
corridors of the "North-Western Hotel," scanning the guests
who thronged them, looking in vain for the original. It was
a *North*-western joke, duly appreciated and atoned for. Mr.
Childs' elegant Art Gallery is one of the popular resorts of
that city. His specialty of stereoscopic views, known as
"Gems of Lake Superior," are in great demand, and lake
tourists who visit Marquette rarely miss the opportunity to
purchase some of these graphic delineations of the great
lake, of which he has the most complete collection. With
only a single assistant to help manage his small sail boat, he
has spent years in cruising along the coasts and into the bays
of Lake Superior, to gather subjects for artistic reproduction.
A passionate lover of nature, with the eye and hand of an
artist true to their vocation, he has early in life won an honor-
able record, and his refined social and gentlemanly qualities
happily commend him to a large circle of friends.

Here we had an introduction to our guides. The first in
mention, Henry St. Arneuld, is the son of a Frenchman;
holding a responsible position in the employ of one of the
large companies engaged in the mining developments of the
Northwest. His mother is a full blood Chippewa squaw.
Henry has all the vivacity, readiness of humor, colloquial

volubility and adaptability to circumstances of his paternal
descent.   But his Indian mother stamped upon him her native
attachment to the wild and unfettered pursuits of her race,
and trade or traffic cannot allure him from them.   He is in
his best element as an exploring agent in the wilderness, or
still more congenial as a guide and boatman over its tortuous
and rapid rivers.

Our other guide was a full-blooded Menominee Indian,
knowing few simple words of English, but ready in his own
and the Chippewa tongue, which we were told are broadly
distinctive.   Henry on the contrary was well posted in both
of his parental tongues, as well as in English, and hence was
our interpreter in the medley of utterances we encountered.

By all rules of expected custom in such cases, our Menominee
should have had a high old Indian name, with half a dozen
links to it, significant of some ferocious achievement.   But we
were shocked, It was simply _Amos Crane!_   It was a reminder
of Byron's respects to one of his literary cotemporaries, who
had trod on his poetical toes:

> "O, Amos Cottle, Phœbus, what a name,
> To fill the sounding trump of future fame!"

Not that the question of fame had ever entered the noddle
of our Menominee.   Sitting in mute, quiet position before the
camp-fire, a champion consumer of fried pork and other eat-
ables, "fame" would have had more charms to him girdled
with a tobacco pouch.   It was the indignity to Indian romance,
in depriving him of his native "barbaric yawp," of a name,
which we felt like resenting.   The only way we could account
for the irrelevancy was, that Amos, filling the position of choir
leader of the Indian Mission among his people, had to be re-
christened, hence another wrong perpetrated upon "Lo! the
poor Indian."   But Amos was a magnificent vocalist, with a
voice almost as flexible as that of the feathered songsters of
his own native wilds.   As we sat in the boat and listened to
his rendering of "Happy Days," and "Nearer my God to
Thee," in his native tongue, there was a charm in it lingering
long in memory.

No. III.

From Marquette to Michagamma lake, about twenty miles distant, there is connection by railroad. The village at that lake, as some of our readers may remember, was devastated by fire about two months ago. It was so furious as to drive a portion of the population into the lake, some of whom, in their efforts to escape from one element by seeking another, were drowned. Our intention was to visit that place, but this disaster changed our direction. Our Secretary of the Navy, Mr. Childs, had procured a boat for us at the Republic iron mines, a few miles south of the lake on the river running from it. We accordingly took the cars from Humboldt, a small settlement about nine miles from Marquette. From this point the Mining Company has built a branch road to the ore beds, about nine miles farther west. While waiting on the platform for an ore train, a familiar countenance greeted us, and we were hailed by an old Poughkeepsie acquaintance, Mr. Frank Allen, son of the late Joseph E. Allen, of this city. The meeting was as pleasant as it was unexpected. He left Poughkeepsie a few years ago, with a slender purse but with a good stock of enterprise and perseverance, and began his business career at the foot of the ladder. He has now a fine store and a post-office commission at Humboldt, and has also just completed and stocked the largest store at Republic.

Our interview was interrupted by the rumbling of cars, which stopped only long enough to receive us and our baggage. As the train was composed only of empty ore cars, we sprang into one of them and took an electric battery nine miles long, bouncing over thick studded inequality of surface, something like Sancho Panza undergoing his blanketing operation. To add to the novelty of the exercise a smart shower began to fall, and the red rust of the ore adhered to us as smoothly as paint to an Indian, so that we presented a very uncivilized spectacle as we made our grand entree into Republic. But costume has no regulation standard at the mines, nor iron nuggets any particular beauty of appearance.

A rough exterior uniformly covers value in the one case, and sometimes among the hardy sons of toil on the other, and the absence of the latest fashions in external apparel furnishes no cause of anxiety.

Iron is king here. Though we have no data at hand of its relative annual value of yield, compared with that of the beds of copper and silver which are found in and about Lake Superior farther north, we infer from what we casually learned that it is second to no other mining interest of this remarkable mineral region. Agents are prospecting for iron ore on government lands, and several new and promising mines have been opened within a few months past. The limits of supply would seem to be bounded only by the availability of manual labor and machinery for extracting it, and the carrying means to navigation.

The lumbering industry has considerable rivalry in commercial enterprise. But it is beginning to feel the effects of comparative exhaustion. Forests contiguous to water-courses have been almost denuded of their pine growth, and we saw little on our route to meet our ideal vision in this respect. Upon this topic a writer in a late issue of the Chicago *Tribune* presents some facts which may interest the reader. He says:

" The present and ever-increasing want of timber demands a general awakening on the subject of tree-growing. New York has lost her maple, walnut and hickory forests. The great Wisconsin forests are in process of rapid destruction. No less than one billion thirty million feet were cut in 1871. Tens of thousands of logs are annually rafted down the Mississippi to Iowa, where they are cut into lumber. Young & Co. have a mill at Clinton, Iowa, that runs two hundred saws, and three-fourths of all the lumber they cut goes to Kansas and Nebraska. In a single year one hundred and eighty-five million feet of Wisconsin logs were cut in Iowa. Ten, or, at most, twenty years from now, not only the Wisconsin, but Michigan and Minnesota forests will be swept away. Fifty thousand acres of Wisconsin timber are cut annually to supply the Kansas and Nebraska markets alone.

There is now left in the whole of the United States, untouched, but one tract of fine timber, consisting of about one-
half of Washington Territory and one-third of Oregon. It is
still a vast scope of land, covered by the magnificent yellow
fir, many trees being three hundred feet high. The Northern Pacific railroad will open up this belt, and when it is
gone, the last of the great American forests will have disappeared. Already exportations from it to China and Japan
have commenced, and it cannot last over ten, or at most
twenty years. It will be for the next half decade our ship
building center, and then where shall we go for our ship-
timber?"*

These are gloomy forebodings, but not worth lying appre-
hensively awake about. When our household or student
lamps were threatened with an eclipse, on account of the
growing scarcity of the big fish which supplied them with oil,
gas came in with an illuminating welcome which in turn is
waning before the advent of electricity. A substitute for timber may be more difficult on many accounts. But to say nothing of coal, its many years successor for heating and culinary uses, it is already beginning to become a " back number "
in building purposes, where security against fire is most essential, and iron is still more conspicuous in shipbuilding.
The worry and alarm of to-day is often the ridicule of the
next decade.

To Capt. Pasco, superintendent of the iron mine at Republic,
we are indebted for many courtesies. He took us over the
works explaining the different varieties of the ore, and the immense machinery by which delivery to the cars is accomplished with very little manual labor. The bulk of ore ex-
tracted is of the magnetic kind, almost pure, and sparkling

---

* Twenty years later, under date of Chicago, February 21, 1893, the
now Secretary of Agriculture at Washington, J. Sterling Morton, is reported as saying: Despite the fact that I should be jubilant over my
recent elevation, I am troubled. Every day that passes sees the timber
producing land of this country reduced by twenty-five thousand acres.
There are but forty million acres of timber left in this country and
at this rate of destruction it will last but a generation.

with its wealth. Trains of fifty or sixty cars are run under a towering elevator, pierced with "shutes," into whose capacious pockets above the ore is dropped by cars descending a railway from the mine, the loaded cars drawing up the empty ones on a parallel railway, by a continuous chain. Each carload of ore represents a value of $40. The company is now shipping from seven hundred to nine hundred tons per day. About one hundred and fifty men are employed in the mines at remunerating wages. There was marked evidence of system and order throughout. Surrounded as the occupation seems to be with exposure to accident, judicious oversight has made such visitations of rare occurrence. A competent physician and surgeon is employed by the company. He has an extensive charge, and does not have to earn his fee over again by cost of mileage in its collection.

No. IV.

Our trip now commences "DOWN THE RAPIDS." While getting ready to leave Republic, a venerable looking Indian approached the shore in a canoe. Its occupants, besides himself, were two red men and a squaw with an infant in her arms. There was a pack of deer skins in the boat, the trophies of a recent hunt. The canoe was just the craft we wanted, and as his place (for he was a chief among his people) was only a few miles down the river and they could easily reach home, we put Henry into a negotiation for its purchase. After a brief Indian confab, Henry informed us that he was unwilling to part with it on any terms — it was a present to him from "the boys" of his tribe, and it wouldn't be right to sell it. We increased the price $5 at different offers, not taking much stock in his alleged scruples, but every proposition was declined, although in a manner which seemed to invite a higher bid. At last we gave Henry an ultimatum at $45. The answer was "make it $50 and you shall have it." The extravagant price was enough to end the chaffer, and we parted from old "Eagle Eye," a temporary convert, at least, to the prevalent opinion here that the Indian is a nuisance.

8

Our paddles struck welcome music as we pushed out into
the stream. The Michaganima river here stretched out into
a spacious bay, upon whose low banks the village of Republic
is built. The dark bold mountain of ore rose in close proximity in a southern parallel to the line of buildings, its surface
offering no lodgment for seed or root. For unnumbered
centuries it has stood unknown to treasure-seekers for its
commercial value. About two years ago the first business
opening was made upon it, and now it is a monthly fortune
to its owners.

The current sent us swiftly along without much aid from
the paddle, and soon we had our first experience in running a
rapid. For some thirty or forty rods the water was in mad
commotion, boiling over the rocks. It did not look interesting,
and we felt a strong desire to go ashore. Amos stood in the
stern, and in commanding tones shouted his orders to Henry
at the bow — "chig-a-bee! chig-a-bee!" or "ah-punt! ah-
punt" — as its different steering was required. Over the
rapids we were whirled in to the smooth waters below, Amos
yelling a grand Indian hulabaloo as we settled into quiet bottom again. For a distance of some two hundred and fifty
miles rapids frequently intervene and are lively zest to boating. In charge of skillful and experienced guides, as we had,
the motion soons becomes a pleasant sensation. Only once
did the experience have an unpleasant result. We had entered
upon a particularly rough and intricate rapid, and as the
boat was lurching upon a submerged rock, Henry thrust his
paddle between it and the boat, and the paddle snapped in
twain like a pipe-stem, dipping a small cataract, completely
sousing the passengers in the first-class cabin. He caught up
a spare paddle in time to save us from further unpleasantness,
and we put for the first convenient camping ground.

The night had a strong touch of December, and we have a
very distinct recollection of a couple of very blue and moody
adventurers, disgusted with all sublunary affairs, standing before a camp-fire, and turning at intervals around, in a drying
and shivering process. Henry also took the little episode to

heart, and denounced the treacherous paddle. Morning, however, brought all things bright. With the new day we passed
into a new atmosphere, and the evening conjurations of ill,
and its sources of disquiet, had taken wing with congenial
darkness.

The feathered game, for which this region is noted, soon attracted our attention. Wild pigeons flitted over us in great
numbers, seeking their feed from the berry bushes which
were in full bearing. Partridges were also around us in
abundance. Amos, whose eye was as keen and piercing as a
hawk's, allowed nothing in the shape of game to escape his
attention. The shores of the river furnished hatching ground
and feed for wild ducks. Fishing was also lively sport. At
favorable places, especially near the inlet of a cold brook, we
found trout in abundance. Black bass abound, and can be
captured in any desirable quantity. There was no necessity
for hunger on the way.

No. V.

Soon after leaving our night's camping ground, on the third
morning of the downward run, we espied a deer, the first we
had seen on the route. He was feeding at the point of a
narrow set off from the main channel, about a hundred yards
distant. The current carried us swiftly past the opening, and
the recognition was apparently mutual, for as we turned back
to the point the buck was also intently watching our movements. Slee had his rifle in readiness, and there was a
moment of expectation as the boat was being brought around
to clear the intervening bushes. "We dreamed of all things
fair,"—especially of a fair, juicy venison steak. But just
as the position was gained for a fair shot, the buck flung up
his caudal appendage defiantly, and we were left in the lurch.
"Death had *not* marked him for his own"—or ours either.
Such a turn of events always leaves one of the interested
parties in an awkward position; but veterans in many a
similar trial are prepared to take it gracefully. Of all the

"back tracks" in life, strewed with blighted hopes, few tax more heavily the philosophy of cheerful resignation.

During the remainder of our excursion down the Michagamma, which occupied about a week, no deer came in sight. This beautiful animal, like the wild fowl of the northern waters, has also its migrating season, when it travels in herds hundreds of miles south to avoid the severity of winter. Its course is usually along the banks of rivers, and Indian and other hunters select favorable points for encampment, and slaughter them by the hundreds. The racks or scaffolding, for drying and curing the venison, were visible in many places along the route. The time of this exodus is generally the latter part of August and through September. We were about two weeks in advance of this season. A scattered few remain through the year in the forests contiguous to the Menominee river and its tributaries, and from these the Indians manage to get their supplies for food and other domestic uses through the summer as well as winter.

Our last camp on the Michigamma was at one side of a beautiful fall, a sheet of foaming water about thirty feet over a rocky ledge and spanned by a charming rainbow. It was admirably picturesque in its thick setting of evergreens. Trout find here congenial haunts in the deep and agitated waters. Below the falls the river spread out in a broad basin, and a few rods farther down it entered at right angles as a tributary of the Menominee river.

Outstretched on our evergreen mattress, with the unceasing voice of many waters in their wild play, lit by an unclouded moon, there was too much of the suggestive history of its surrounding changes in the lapse of centuries, for sleep to become a ready visitor. To the lover of wilderness scenery we know of none more charming than is presented in and about the numerous falls of the Michigamma and Menominee rivers, of which there are six worthy of special note within two or three days' boating; one at the junction of the two rivers just named, Big Poquinessey, Little Poquinessey, the Twin Falls (not far apart, and so called from their resemblance to each other) and one other, the gem of the series, whose distinctive name we have forgotten. They vary in descent from twenty to forty feet, carrying a dense volume of water which projecting rocks churn into whiteness over the entire surface, and presenting so many points of attraction that the vision tires with the overstrain.

The carries through the forests to the foot of these falls vary from a quarter to two and a half miles; and as our camp equipments and boat were so bulky as to make a return trip necessary, the progress on the long portages were necessarily slow. The end of the first long carry brought us to the foot of one of the falls we have mentioned, and while our guides were after the second load, we pushed out in the boat to the entrance of a spring brook. Although the midday sun was lighting the spot, we took twenty-three trout, varying from a quarter to three-quarters of a pound, in less than an hour. Slee's tackling parted as he was bringing in an old settler, almost in reach of an arm outstretched to take it in out of the wet.

We were getting anxious to capture a deer, and thus furnish our commissary department with a change. Our guides informed us that about half a mile west there were three small lakes connected by narrow channels, which was a favorite hunting ground of the Indians. We carried across to this place and stayed two nights, the only exception to the daily folding of tent and resuming our journey. We saw no signs of deer, but black bass and pickerel fishing was lively.

Passing a beautiful island which divided the Menominee river midway, Henry gave us an Indian legend of long ago, which is still religiously held among the Menominees. An Indian maiden was suffering from some indisposition for which the tradition of that people required her temporary seclusion. She was, therefore, left alone in a hut on an island, some distance from the rest of her tribe. But one morning she was sought, and could not be found. Months passed without any sign of the missing maiden. At length a hunting party, returning late at night, while passing this island saw the lost maiden in vivid reality, standing upon the bank. They addressed her, but received no answer. They landed, but the vision receded, and as they advanced it disappeared. The verity of the legend is unquestioned among her people, who believe that the mute maiden vouchsafes at times her spirit-presence to those who are satisfied with the opportunity of seeing her at a respectful distance and with sealed lips.

We also learned from the same authority that the Chippewas and Menominees have their spirit-mediums, and Henry dilated at length his personal witness of a scene which they call "The Shaking of the Tent." Certain old men among them, respected for their wisdom, are the chosen receptacles of this "influence." According to his account, one of these mediums, known by an appellation which was too intricate for a short memory to retain, enters alone a tent, the stout center pole of which is fastened deep in the ground, and throwing himself prostrate, commences a wild chant or incantation. Soon the pole of the tent begins to vibrate, at first slowly, but increasing in extent and rapidity of motion with an agitation which no mortal arms could produce. Several voices were also heard in the Indian chant. As each additional voice joined in, a loud crash was heard, indicating the arrival of a reinforcement. The chief spirit spokesman seemed to be an old chief, and when asked as to the nature of his revelations, Henry replied, that 'it was advice how to live a good life. Henry said he had often heard of these demonstrations among the Indians, but was utterly sceptical until he was a witness of what he had related. He spoiled the solemnity of his narrative, however, by adding. "that the scene affected him so powerfully that he roared with laughter." We confess to have sympathized with him at the fun of the circus. But if mortal vision is to be purged of its obstructions, so as to inlet this new perception of spirit possibilities, we should prefer to take it as an Indian dose rather than through any other agency.

No. VI.

The first Indian settlement we reached on the Menominee is at a place called "Bad Water." not from any peculiarity in its taste, but from its general roughness. The Indian name is *We-bo-juano*, or Narrowing of the Rapids. There were a few log shanties and bark wigwams. We made a morning visit, and as our guides were acquainted with them, and business didn't seem to be driving on their part, we handed around cigars and had a chatty smoke, enjoying the Indian talk, if we didn't understand it. The squaws and pappooses all had a squalid, untidy appearance, and their garments were an odd compromise between savage and civilized styles. We looked in vain for the romantic "Leather-stocking" picture our fancy had painted. There was not enough of Indian scare about them to make the situation interesting. The fact occurred to us that when we were informed at Marquette that we should find nobody but Indians on the route, we furtively made inquiry whether white visitors straying into their territory were likely to find hospitality and kindly reception. We felt the ridiculous nature of the apprehension involved in that inquiry as we sat among these degenerate aborigines. They are evidence, at least in this region, that the traditional red men of old New England times have disappeared from forest, lake and river. Among the tribes living more remote from the pale faces, and possessing pride and strength enough to keep up their race individuality, doubtless there is more of the old Indian stamina left.

We had another object, beside the exchange of visiting courtesies, in making this call. We had seen from the river a new canoe, and concluded to make another effort for a trade. When the Indian talk with our guides had begun to slacken, probably from exhaustion of all the gossip about the outer world, we told Henry to sound the "big Indian," who, we learned, was the maker and owner of it. The canoe was pronounced by our guide to be composed of a perfect piece of bark of the best birch, and as good a craft of the kind as we

could find on the river. But the old man was not in selling
mood, especially as we proposed to throw in our boat as part of
the consideration. At this point of the trade a third party appeared. An old squaw came out of a wigwam, leaning upon
a long stick, with a wrinkled countenance and parchment
skin, as if marked by a century, and long black hair loosely
flowing — a very suggestive "Meg Merriles." She learned
from Henry the nature of the discussion. And then commenced an animated talk with the old Indian, whose squaw
she was. We should have mentioned that he wore a large black
patch, covering almost his entire nose, and tied around the back
of his head. Henry had learned the secret of this fixture, and
informed us that the squaw had bit off the lower portion of
that facial ornament, in a recent domestic unpleasantness.
She evidently was the boss diplomat and favored our proposi-
tion. It did not take her long to bring the chief to terms.
Curiosity to learn her age, led me to ask the information
through our interpreter. I saw from her countenance that
she parried the question, with the usual spirit'of her sex when
a meddling masculine asks it. She would have been a lively
customer for a census-taker. After some bantering between
them, she said she did not know how old she was, nor where
she was born, curtly adding, that I needn't be so inquisitive
about it, as her hair wasn't as gray as mine! My curiosity
suddenly abated.

The canoe bargain having been settled, the finishing process on the boat (" pitching the seams," by applying a compo-
sition of melted spruce gum and grease to the seams where the
bark is cut to shape it, and is then sewed together by a very
strong fibrous root) was proceeded with. This work uniformly
devolves upon the squaws, and three of them took it in hand,
superintended by the old squaw. The Indians squatted
around smoking their pipes, and we found ourselves in a
novel circle, where the dignity of "the lords of creation"
was asserted in the most primitive, aboriginal style. The entire population of " Bad Water" gathered at the river side,
where the canoe was launched. As we were ready to pro-

ceed on our journey, I jocosely suggested to Henry to invite
the old squaw to accompany us. To our dismay she assented,
and started for the canoe. A broad grin overspread the countenance of her wedded companion, indicating a full assent on
his part, but we made an ungallant and hasty retreat from the
dilemma, leaving a slighted squaw shaking her fist at us.

Proceeding down the river a few miles, we camped at a
bluff, adjoining one of the falls to which allusion has already
been made. While getting things in readiness for the night,
Amos caught sight of a deer feeding in the water, about a
quarter of a mile below us. Supper was soon despatched,
and taking Amos to manage the canoe, Slee went in search of
the animal, while Henry remained with me by the camp-fire,
calculating the chances. They had been absent but a short
time when we heard the report of a gun, and not long after a
second discharge. We watched with confidence that the
cruise was successful, and in about an hour the canoe was at
the camp with a fine large doe. The second shot was made
at a large buck, standing out some distance in the stream, but
the gathering darkness made the mark uncertain, and he
escaped. In the morning our guides rose early to dress the
deer, and the sun was not yet in sight, when Henry called
me up, saying there were three deer on the beach just below
the camp. Going to the edge of the bluff, we beheld as pretty
a scene as any hunter could wish. On the broad, sandy margin of the basin below the falls, about twenty rods from us, a
buck, doe and fawn were frolicking in high glee. We watched
their play for some time, behind our bushy screen. A suggestion from Henry to shoot was valiantly resisted, as our
supply of venison was now superabundant. A clap of the
hands sent them bouncing into the sheltering forest, to become the prey of some more needy hunters before a returning
summer. We had evidently reached a favorite feeding
ground for deer, for between our arrival at evening of that
day and ten o'clock next morning, on our way down, we
counted eleven, and were fully supplied for the remainder of
our sojourn in the woods.

No. VII.

One kind of fish frequently seen in the Menominee river we have not yet mentioned. It was the last place where we should expect to find sturgeon, yet they are here in great numbers, swimming lazily up stream in search of spawning ground. All we saw were much smaller than those which inhabit the Hudson river, not exceeding four feet in length. Sturgeon river, which runs into the Menominee some seventy-five miles south of its source, receives its name from this fish, and some distance up this tributary is Sturgeon falls, where natural obstructions bound their further ascent.

At these falls a lumber company have a large farm, from which it gets the supplies for the laborers and stock employed in winter lumbering.

At White Rapids we reached another Indian settlement, the Indian name *We-bo-baco*, derived from the falling of the waters over rocks of a light color, resembling marble. Some attention is here paid by the Indians to cultivation, and small patches of corn and potatoes were in thrifty condition. We paddled up to a log shanty on the bank of the river, where an old Indian was seated, smoking his pipe. He was an uncle of Amos, whom he had not seen for six years. The interview was formal and quiet, their short utterances being broken by repeated whiffs of smoke. One after another the other members of the family joined the circle as listeners, after a handshake of recognition. In the mean time we sat in the canoe in the full pour of a melting midday sun, wishing that the stream of kindred affection might rush into a like broiling flood and exhaust itself. But all things have an end, even an aboriginal reunion of long scattered members. The old man brought out as a present a pair of venerable antlers, to which was added about a peck of cucumbers, raised in his garden. We lightened our cargo by leaving our supplies of venison, flour, pork and other articles, which the nearness to the end of our river run made no longer necessary.

Our tent was pitched that night, for the last of the trip, on the banks of these pleasant waters. The morning opened in rare beauty, and as we floated with easy speed down the current, requiring but little effort of the paddle, the situation afforded an agreeable sensation of change with rest. Birds, some of beautiful plumage, were at their morning vocation, charming the eye and tuneful to the ear. Amos was in most exuberant mood, glowing over with his sacred mission songs, in which he was joined by Henry, who strove to make up in his appreciation of melody what he lacked in devotional sentiment.

As we have already remarked, the Menominee river is the border line between Michigan and Wisconsin, once the new territory of the "far West," but now furnishing their own increase of population to the frontier settlements. They are both still rich in their mineral, and comparatively so in their forest, wealth, and contribute largely in these staples to the supply of middle and eastern markets. As the lumber needed for commercial demand ceases to furnish remunerative occupation, business enterprise will fall back upon the apparently inexhaustible deposits of the different ores, which are as yet comparatively untouched by mining implements. While there are so many more inviting fields in the West for the hand of agriculture, offering a greater yield to less toil, it must be years before these river banks give evidence of prosperous farmers' homes. Here and there, as we progressed toward the mouth of the river, were seen the humble abodes of settlers, who had opened a spot in the wilderness for their household goods, where, if their lives are not filled with the rounded measure of a more abundant social life, at least have their compensation in a more robust existence and greatly diminished sources of social disquiet, meeting Dr. Goldsmith's idea. "If few their joys, their wants are also few." And I was deeply interested in the explanation of the situation, between a couple among whom we happened to find ourselves. The husband, who was originally from Maine, had not overcome his longing to go back to his old social life, and plead as a reason for it, that their children, who were numerous around them, would thus have a better opportunity for education, and to become somebody. But the wife had no sympathy for such a change. She said they got along comfortably, raised all they needed and had a surplus to carry out to market, and the children were out of the reach of temptation. Who will say that her philosophy was not the correct one in view of the fact which we subsequently learned, that thirst for alcohol had formerly been her husband's failing, and that here, in the solitude of Nature, that terrible destroyer of home and its happiness found no congenial lodgment? The returning ways to the dram shop were more frightful to her than the dreariness of her wilderness abode, or the deprivation of community comforts and advantages. The highest forms of moral heroism and the noblest examples of self-sacrifice have many a field of daily exercise, unnoted save by the All Seeing Eye.

Besides these occasional little clearances, whose extent could almost be taken in by a sweep of the eye, we passed two farms on a large scale, one of them stretching along the bank of the river three or four hundred acres in extent, with large and comfortable looking buildings. The crops on it were luxuriant, especially the oats, which in stalk and heading I have rarely seen equaled. We were obliged to cross a portion of it to carry boat and baggage round a rocky shoal in the river. A large turnip field, well fruited, as Col. Sellers might say, was trodden thickly with the fresh tracks of feeding deer, which had found the presence of civilized life attractive at least to one sense.

The stretch of wilderness and water, through which our excursion of about four hundred miles had led us, has unquestionably superior attractions for the gun and rod over the North Woods of our own State; yet it is less trod by the feet of hunter and angler. We met only with a solitary couple on our long route, and they were going only a short distance. But in the feature of scenery it is out of sight in the comparison. It has nothing of the grandeur of mountain ranges,

or the frequent relief of bubbling icy springs, which at almost
every depression in the earth's surface mark the Adirondack
regions, and which border by the one and feed with the other,
its beautiful and unequaled lakes. In these essentials of
perfection to wilderness scenery it is tame and deficient.

No. VIII.

As we approached within a few miles of the outlet of the
river, we were struck by the continuous stretch of bare and
blackened trunks of trees, extending for miles on both sides
of the track of the great Peshtigo fire two years ago. One
hastily constructed tenement, built since the disaster, had its
family reminder of the fire, as we learned soon after. About
three miles above Menominee city we found the river closely
blocked with logs, which compelled us to take our canoe
and baggage ashore and find a team conveyance. Leaving
our guides, I started with Slee to foot it to the city to pro-
cure aid. We had not proceeded far when we were overtaken
by a man and his wife in a small one-horse wagon, loaded for
market. He insisted that there was room enough for us, and
kindly assured us that if his wagon had been a little larger
he would have taken in boat and baggage also. Getting into
conversation, we learned that his name was Joseph Begieu,
and he informed us that he lived in the house we have just
referred to, and that on the morning of the fire he started
early with his two little boys and a daughter to go to Menominee city. On his return he had got within a mile of
the river when the air became filled with smoke, and he
heard the roaring of the approaching fire He hurried his
horse, but the flames were soon sweeping all around him, and
he was obliged to abandon his wagon and pick his way along
in less exposed places. The dense smoke was suffocating,
and the rush of flames so near that their clothes at times
caught fire. He encouraged his children in efforts to reach
the river, and when the heat and smoke were at times so in-
tense that they felt like giving up to the situation, he dug
holes in the sand with his hands, and told them to lie down

9

and place their mouths over the opening. As the rush of the hot current changed to another point they rose and struggled on again. In this condition, scorched and nearly strangled, they finally reached the river and plunged into the protecting waters. The fire was burning fiercely in the direction of his home, and he expected to find his wife and remaining children victims to it.

His wife then told her thrilling story. She was alone with two little children, one a sick baby. She was startled by the roar of the fire, and in her anxiety for her helpless charge became almost paralyzed. Her hope was that the fire might pass to one side, and she watched in agony of apprehension as it reached out in every direction. Fortunately she was not far from the river, and rousing herself to the necessity of the situation, she caught up her sick child and leading the other, they also found refuge in the water, where not long after she was joined by her husband and children who had come up the river in a boat. In the overwhelming joy of such a deliverance and reunion, it concerned them lightly at the time, that all their worldly effects were in smoking ruins. Truth is indeed often stranger than fiction. It seems like a wild, wonderful story, but I have related their account of it, and had no reason to question their veracity.

At Menominee we found comfortable quarters at the public house of Bush Brothers. Mr. Bush despatched a team for our canoe and effects, and the snug little craft was put in the hands of the express company for home transportation.

Menominee is a smart growing little sawdust city. It abounds in saw-mills, and even the streets are paved with sawdust. On the Wisconsin side of the river, directly opposite, extending backward from Green Bay, is Marionette, a thrifty town of about the same size.

A number of Indians get some sort of a livelihood here, just at this season, by picking berries for market. We saw a company of them riding on their small ponies, and dressed in full Indian costume, more like the genuine article than any we had seen. One of them, who dropped into the hotel for a few moments, was a study for an artist. He had leggins and moccasins, and a loose outer garment of dressed deerskin. With the exception of his headgear this completed his costume. He was over six feet in height, and carried a remarkably long rifle. As he stepped off in long strides, trailing his rifle, he was more like a dusky Micawber, content with his situation, and ready for whatever might turn up, than a Logan mourning the departure of his kindred and the faded glories of his race.

We are sorry in closing our veritable narrative to be compelled to add, that the high appreciation we had held of the steadiness of Amos against bibulous temptation was doomed to a temporary eclipse. His red-skin brethren at the end of the route seduced him into a spiritual pow-wow, and Amos came out of it "tighter than a brick." A contemporaneous writer recently summed up the general failing of the Indian in this wise :

"Historians the wide world over will be shocked to learn, that the Chabbaquidule tribe of Indians are extinct, the last representative thereof having slept the sleep of death at Martha's Vineyard last week. His virtuous memory is embalmed by a local chronicle in the statement, that he was a professor of religion, a regular attendant upon camp meeting services, and an inveterate drunkard."

From our knowledge of the entire abstinence of Amos from any thing intoxicating while in our employ, and from the testimony of others, we had reason to believe that this was a very rare occurrence in his case. He came out of his debauch penitent and poorer. We had purchased for our guides their railroad tickets homeward, in addition to their $3 a day each from the time of leaving Marquette. We parted from them with kindly interest, appreciating their skill and faithfulness, and turned in a different direction homeward.

And so winds up our remembrances of adventure and sight-seeing DOWN THE RAPIDS of the Michagamma and Menominee rivers.

BIBLE LESSONS.

Father Forgive Them. LUKE, XXIII, 34.

With meek submission He endured the base
   Indignities of His unfeeling foes;
Though doomed each moment to some new disgrace,
   No malediction from His breast arose —
No withering curse upon the heads of those,
   Who were pursuing with vindictive scorn
Their persecution, even to life's close;
   With lofty resignation all was borne,
And placid, fervent as a mother's prayers,
   When for her offspring heavenly gifts they sue,
His dying voice a message upward bears —
   " Forgive them for they know not what they do."

On heathen pages we shall search in vain
   For aught that gives a sentiment like this —
Forgiveness — love — triumphing over pain,
   The authors of His sufferings to bless —
Sweet mercy even in the hour of death;
   Its spirit is divine — it breathes of heaven —
'Tis the peculiar essence of that faith
   To which His life a sacrifice was given.
He who will bring unto this noble theme
   A heart inquiring for the heavenly road,
Must with the Roman officer exclaim —
   Convinced — " This truly was the Son of God."

Salem, Mass., 1834.

The Cedars of Lebanon.

"The books, prophetic, poetic and historical, of the Old Testament abound in references to Lebanon, which supplied the timber for Solomon's magnificent temple and palaces. . . . The famous B'Sherrah grove is three-quarters of a mile in circumference, and contains about four hundred trees. Perhaps a dozen of these are very old; the largest, sixty-three feet in girth, is thought to have attained the age of two thousand years." — *Encyclopedia.*

Majestic monarchs of the forest kind,
   Thy regal crests for ages thou hast reared,
In bold defiance to the mountain wind;
   Thy realm-o'ershadowing branches, still unseared
By the stern ravager of earthly things,
   And mocking the decay widespread around,
As when o'er Israel reigned her native kings,
   Yet to the whisperings of the breeze resound.

The lawless Arab deems thou art divine,
   And climbs the rocky heights of Lebanon,
To offer to thee on thy mountain shrine
   The homage which belongs to God alone.
Thy dateless birth uplifts the soul with awe,
   And stirs those deep emotions of the heart,
Which nearer to their God His creatures draw,
   And to their minds a holy glow impart.

From off the heritage o'erlooked by thee,
   Successive generations have been swept —
Contending armies, with a sanguine sea,
   The plains outspreading far below have steeped,
Since first thy forms into existence sprang;
   And they, the chosen messengers of God
To Israel — the sacred seers who sang
   Of thee — long since have mouldered 'neath the sod.

Thou hast beheld Judea's glory wane,
   The sceptre wrenched from her enfeebled hands,
And seest the curse-bound few who still remain,
   Submissive vassals in their fathers' lands.

Where the Shechinah once resplendent shone,
　　The lamps of Islamism brightly glow,
And of her boasted Temple, not a stone
　　Remains, her famed magnificence to show.
But thou art still the same; of all that lived,
　　When first on earth appeared the heavenly LIGHT,
EMMANUEL, thou only hast survived
　　To see its beams dispelling error's night.

Salem. Mass., 1834.

The Doomed City.

MARK, XIII, 19. — *For in those days shall be affliction, such as was not from the beginning of the creation, which God created unto this time, neither shall be.*

The sentence had gone forth, and now had come
　　The time, when nothing earthly could withhold
The heaven-forsaken city, from the doom
　　By Him, whose word can never fail, foretold —
When desolation's tide was to be rolled
　　O'er the devoted Queen of Palestine,
And War its crimson banners foul unfold,
　　Till Death should, over-gorged, his work resign.

Around — the instruments of Providence —
　　Were leagued the legions of all-conquering Rome,
Hemming their victims in a space from whence
　　Escape was none — their only chance the tomb,
Or to be borne as captives, at the car
　　Of victory, subjected to the mock
Of their rude captors — in some land afar
　　From their loved home, to wear a bondsman's yoke.

Within — the breasts of the besotted race
　　Were rife with envy, discord, tumult, hate,
The busy workers of their own disgrace,
　　And rushing headlong on their willful fate;

The ghastly form of Famine stalked abroad,
　　And laid its withering spell on every heart,
Till Nature was outraged, and hunger gnawed,
　　With fiendish rage, the dearest ties apart.

Above — terrific, fearful, many a sign
'　Mysterious and portentous o'er them glared —
Emblems of boundless slaughter — wrath divine,
　　To those who had its retributions dared.
Unheeded were these tokens; still they fought,
　　Insatiate thirsting for each other's blood,
Increasing crime, regardless of the thought
　　They soon must meet the presence of their God.

She fell at last.　The Roman drove the plough
　　O'er the foundations of the blackened scene,
And leaving nought but Nature's hand to show
　　Where once Jerusalem, the proud, had been.
HIS WORD IS TRUTH.　All things coöperate
　　To accomplish whatsoever He has willed,
And madness 'tis to doubt — or soon or late —
　　That all which He declares will be fulfilled.
Salem, Mass., 1834.

" Our Father Who Art in Heaven."

1 PETER, 5-7 —Casting all your care upon Him, for He careth for you.

　　He careth for us! — then our faith
　　　　Should ever keep us from despair;
　　No doubts should trouble one who hath
　　　　The shield of the Almighty's care.

　　He careth for us! — welcome then,
　　　　Our Father, be Thy discipline,
　　Forbid that we should e'er complain,
　　　　And keep, oh keep, our souls from sin.

He careth for us! — all things move
　　In joyful concert for the good
Of those who manifest their love,
　　By lives of holiness, to God.

He careth for us! — and when Death
　　Shall lay on us its icy hand,
He'll crown with an immortal wreath
　　His children, in a heavenly land.

Salem, Mass., 1834.

"Fear Not."

GENESIS, XXI, 16, 17. — And she went and sat her down over against him a good way off — for she said, Let me not see the death of the child. And she sat over against him, and lifted up her voice and wept. And God heard the voice of the lad; and the angel of the Lord called to Hagar out of heaven, and said unto her, fear not.

Beneath the shrubs she laid her child
　　And turned her from his suffering glance,
She could not bear th' expression wild
　　That settled on his countenance.

She wept — the tears of agony
　　From the outcast handmaiden burst,
To think her Ishmael must die
　　By the slow-torturing of thirst.

She wept, that she must bid adieu
　　Forever to her only son,
And henceforth sorrowing pursue
　　Her weary pilgrimage alone.

But hark! a heavenly voice conveys
　　Delightful tidings to her ear —
"What aileth thee? fear not," it says,
　　Thy God is with thee even here.

The shade hath vanished from her eyes;
　The crystal fount which now appears,
A life-restoring aid supplies —
　She weeps, but these are joyful tears.

So, oft, when life's dark scenes amid,
　We sink o'erwhelmed with deep distress —
And grieve, as lonely Hagar did,
　While in Beersheba's wilderness —

We too an angel's voice may hear,
　Which all anxieties dispel —
Entreating us to banish fear,
　And showing us a "living well."

Salem, Mass., 1834.

Peter's Trial Hour.

Luke, xxii, 61. —And the Lord turned and looked upon Peter.

He looks on his abandoned Lord,
　Who stands with shackled limb,
And though His lips breathe not a word,
　His eyes are fixed on him; —
It is enough — that searching gaze
　Hath thrilled through Peter's frame,
And the tear of bitterness betrays
　The boaster's grief and shame.

So, many a virtuous decree
　Our hearts to action move,
But in the hour of trial, we,
　Like Peter, faithless prove.
Yet still the same omniscient eyes
　On our transgressions rest,
And well — who thus his Lord denies —
　If tears his grief attest.

Salem, Mass., 1834.

Wrestling with the Angel.

" Millions of spiritual creatures walk the earth,
   Unseen, both when we wake and when we sleep." — *Milton*.

Genesis, XXXII, 24–31. And Jacob was left alone; and there wrestled a man with him until the breaking of the day. And when he saw he prevailed not, he touched the hollow of his thigh, and the hollow of Jacob's thigh was out of joint as he wrestled with him. And he said, let me go, for the day breaketh. And he said, I will not let thee go, except thou bless me. And he said unto him, What is thy name ? And he said, Jacob. And he said, thy name shall be called no more Jacob, but Israel: for as a prince thou hast power with God and with men, and hast prevailed. And Jacob asked him, and said, Tell me, I pray thee, thy name; and he said, Wherefore is it that thou dost ask after my name ? And he blessed him there.

Night closed upon the scene at Mahanaim.
A suppliant, Jacob sent his mission forth,
Armed heavily with the ministry of peace:
The thronging memories of the past replaced
The parting forms of kindred and of friends,
And glorious promises to him and his,
Of large possessions and a numerous seed,
Could scarce suppress his fears of Esau's ire.

Jacob remained alone with troubled thoughts,
As rolled the brook 'twixt him and all of earth.
But lo ! a shining form the silence breaks,
Hailed by the patriarch as a pledge of good,
With whom he wrestled till the break of day;
The blessing, seen by faith, he earnest sought,
Nor yielded, though the angel, for release,
His sinew shrank with touch of mighty power,
And left him halting on a weakened thigh.

Oh, splendid gift by perseverance won !
Not Jacob now, but Israel, pregnant name
Of power prevailing both with God and man.
" Thy name," says Jacob. " Wherefore that to thee ? "
He blessed him there; and Esau's kindly face
Came with unselfish and forgiving grace.

So may we wrestle for divine support,
When in the lonely walks of life we wait,
And apprehensions of some coming ill
Lead us to feel how frail and weak we are;
So see in all our Father's trial scenes,
A watching angel urging us to zeal,
That we may win the needed gift of grace,
And turn the darkness to celestial light.
Nor idly questioning the helper's name,
While his credentials in the gift we see.
So like our Master, when the Tempter's power
He foiled by sure reliance on God's WORD,
Our work well done, a blessing like shall come
And angel strength be ministered to us.

Poughkeepsie, Sept. 6, 1857.

The Soul's Rest.

MATTHEW, XI, 28–30. Come unto me, all ye that labor, and are heavy laden, and I will give you rest. Take my yoke upon you and learn of me; for I am meek and lowly in heart, and ye shall find rest unto your souls. For my yoke is easy and my burden is light.

Ho ! weary one, estranged from peace,
  By sin's dark burden sadly pressed,
Joy ! for a Saviour brings release,
  And from thy sorrows flee for rest.

Take up His yoke and learn of Him
  The beauty of a holy life,
Whose glorious crown will ne'er grow dim —
  Victor o'er elemental strife.

Lowly and meek, He stooped to earth
  And took our human nature on,
And, like for Jew and Gentile birth,
  Rest for the soul sublimely won.

Easy His yoke, His burden light,
   He doth a royal sceptre wield,
Where love and majesty unite,
   And solace in all trials yield.

"Rest for the soul!" ye stricken child
   Of mortal mould, when faint ye tread,
Where roll life billows dark and wild,
   Lift to this Friend thy drooping head.

Tried by all woes of mortal lot,
   A man of sorrows and of grief,
He knows our weaknesses, and what
   Is best designed to bring relief.

Nor only through the conflicts here,
   Are Christian soldiers richly blest,
Beyond the confines of this sphere,
   For them remains eternal rest.

Rest, such as blissful angels feel,
   While vision-tranced with folded wing,
Their golden harps sweet cadence tell
   Of Him, from whom all blessings spring.
Poughkeepsie, Sept. 13, 1857.

The Numbering of Israel.

2 SAMUEL, XXIV-2.—For the king said to Joab, the captain of the host which was with him, go now through all the tribes of Israel, from Dan even to Beersheba, and number ye the people, that I may know the number of the people.

Go count the people — I would know
   Their number — said the monarch proud —
Fling David's banner to the foe,
   Exultant o'er a mighty crowd.

From Dan to Beersheba then sped,
   Obedient to the royal word,
Captains of host, by Joab led,
   And numbered those who drew the sword.

Ah! subtle tempter, how thy plot
   Hath stirred the Hebrew monarch's pride —
Jehovah's outstretched arm forgot,
   In *numbers* now doth he confide.

Oh! weak distrust of sovereign care,
   Oh! self-reliant Hebrew king,
Thy numbers soon the grave shall share,
   Thy pride become a poisoned sting.

" *What choose ye?* " was the voice of God,
   " *Into Thy hand oh let us fall,*"
Then passed the pestilential rod,
   And echoed loud Death's harvest call.

In vain are walls and bulwarks high,
   An arm of flesh how blindly vain,
Salvation only draweth nigh
   To him who owns Jehovah's reign.

In Thee is everlasting strength,
   Nor ever faileth Thy decree,
In perfect peace Thou'lt keep at length
   The way of him who rests on Thee.

Worship with Thee acceptance finds,
   Though few the suppliant knee may bend,
And serve Thy praise obedient minds,
   Though no proud temple walls ascend.

Trust in the Lord, the moral is,
   Whatever may betide us here —
Earth and its fulness all are His,
   Nor ever should his servants fear.

Poughkeepsie, Oct. 4, 1857.
   10

The Angel of the Sepulchre.

MARK, XVI, 5-6. — And entering into the sepulchre, they saw a young man sitting on the right side, clothed in a long white garment ; and they were affrighted. And he saith unto them, be not affrighted ; ye seek Jesus of Nazareth, which was crucified ; He is risen, He is not here ; behold the place where they laid Him.

The risen sun on First Day morn
   Shone o'er the Saviour's garden tomb,
As came the Marys, sad and lorn,
   Bearing sweet spices and perfume.

With anxious hearts, the Lord they loved
   They sought, and found at early hour
The stone was from the doorway moved,
   Though all untouched by mortal power.

They entered now the rock-hewn way —
   Why do their pulses wildly stir!
There sat in glorious array,
   The angel of the sepulchre.

No lifeless form is outstretched there,
   To need the Marys' kind intent —
Triumphant now — they only share
   The tomb with angel visitant.

"Be not afraid!" Oh! blessed word,
   From lips of white-robed messenger —
Be not afraid, ye seek the Lord,
   Behold! He is no longer here.

Bear to His friends the gladsome news,
   That death had yielded up his might,
And Christ, rejected of the Jews,
   Brings life, immortal life, to light !

The cross and tomb, their work now done,
   " *The heel has bruised the serpent's head,*"
More than was lost Emmanuel won,
   By angel voices heralded.

Thus when life's trial scenes appear,
   Lest from the truth our footsteps err,
By faith's clear utterance may we hear
   The angel of the sepulchre.

Poughkeepsie, Oct. 11, 1857.

Prayer.

The prayer of faith to the burdened breast
   Affords a calm and sweet relief,
For its heavenly influence lulls to rest
   The vain desires whose end is grief.

How great the privilege to raise
   The aspirations of the soul,
And offer up the heartfelt praise
   To power and love that life control.

The bright, alluring scenes of life
   While thus engaged dim not the sight,
Nor worldly din, nor passion's strife,
   Appear to cloud the heavenly light.

Its mild, subduing influence sends
   A holy thrill into the breast,
Its soothing balm a healing lends
   To cure the soul by sin oppressed.

And dear is such commune to those
   Who pine beneath misfortune's load,
For far above all earthly woes
   It lifts the heart in peace to God.

There is in prayer a blessed spell
   For our relief most richly given;
Its hopes are from a living well
   Whose fountain-source is found in heaven.

Salem, Mass., 1834.

MISCELLANEOUS.

To a Red Breast Songster.

I hear at dawn thy caroling,
Thou sweetest songster of the spring,
As up to heaven thy morning prayer
Is borne upon the silent air.

The varying cadence of thy song
With tuneful glee thou dost prolong,
Dispensing from thy perch on high
A spirit-stirring minstrelsy.

Thou sendest out in each wild note
Of gratitude that swells thy throat,
Devotion's melody; a lay
Calling the soul from earth away.

So constantly, at morn and even,
Thou warblest forth the "airs of heaven,"
Thou seem'st commissioned from the skies
To teach us where *our* hearts should rise.

And though I cannot lift a strain,
As pure as thine, from earthly stain,
My voice I'd learn from thee to raise,
At morn and eve, my God to praise.

Salem, Mass., 1834.

Leaving Home.

" First partings form a lesson hard to learn." —L. E. L.

The day, preparing for its flight,
  Had robed itself in twilight's guise,
(Bringing that hour of sober light
  When thought takes wing and backward flies,
And we trace through each departed year
  The various links in being's chain,
Dwelling on those to remembrance dear,
  And living their pleasures o'er again,)
When alone walked forth a youthful bride,
  To take a lingering, parting gaze
On scenes with memory close allied,
  The home of many halcyon days.

The heart will wind itself around
  The objects of its watchfulness —
And keenly feels the sad rebound
  Of broken links and lost caress.
Each shrub and flower that she had reared
  With much of anxious tender care,
Ne'er had so fragrantly appeared
  As at that hour, nor bloomed so fair.
Through bowers endeared by time she roved,
  Her heart with sadness deeply fraught —
At every turn some thing long loved
  Was linked with retrospective thought.

The grove-crowned hill — the winding brook —
  The feathery brood that warbled nigh —
Seemed each to claim a parting look,
  Seemed each to ask a parting sigh ;
And when from earth her eyes would roam,
  To sky of clear cerulean hue,

She thought that o'er another home
　　It could not wear so deep a blue.
Not all the hopes that mutual love
　　Can waken in the youthful breast,
Could with their magic spell remove
　　The weight that on her spirits pressed.

A harder task was she to learn,
　　As morning opened on the scene;
She was henceforth from those to turn,
　　On whom she had been wont to lean
For all affection could confer —
　　For guidance, counsel, sympathy —
From those who had watched over her
　　With love, almost idolatry ;
To break time-hallowed intimacies —
　　For distant lands her home to leave,
Where there were none but stranger faces
　　A smile of welcoming to give.

We cannot form an earthly tie
　　That calls not for some sacrifice ;
How oft in love's bright hour a sigh
　　Of fond regret will softly rise,
To chill the warmth of its caress —
　　The thought of all we must forsake
Obscuring half its loveliness,
　　And causing us from bliss to wake.

But time will dry the parting tear,
　　And blot its memory from the mind ;
Like all that come 'twill disappear,
　　And leave no lasting trace behind.
E'en life's last parting fails to leave
　　A cureless wound upon the heart ;
Time brings a balm to those who grieve,
　　Allaying sorrow's keenest smart.

Our purest joys have some bleak shade,
　　Alloyed by Providence, 'twould seem,
That we may never be betrayed
　　Into forgetfulness — or deem
The human soul — that deathless spark —
　　Can e'er again an Eden find,
Until for heaven it shall embark,
　　And reach the home for it designed ;
That home where partings all shall cease,
　　Nor blight nor end its joys shall know,
Where all shall know that " perfect peace,"
　　(Our Father's word) that He'll bestow.

Salem, Mass., 1834.

Desertion.

Where are the friends who worshipped thee
　　When thou wert fortune's child?
No longer now the crowd I see
　　That on thee kindly smiled,
When wealth and fashion round thee cast
Their fickle charms — too bright to last.

No longer flattery's serpent-tone
　　Beguiles thy listening ear ;
Away the golden charms have flown
　　Which made thee once so dear ;
And flattery never homage paid
Where frowning fortune cast its shade.

Adversity's unerring test,
　　Can only friendship prove,
And never yet hath it suppressed
　　Disinterested love :
And it hath left thee, oh ! how few !
Of all that fond and flattering crew.

Thou moved among them robed in light,
  Eclipsing their dull rays,
And now that drear misfortune's night
  Hath changed thee to their gaze,
With unconcern they think of thee
Nor care thy altered lot to see.

Turn from th' unlovely thoughts that crowd
  In sadness on thy mind —
Let other hopes dispel this cloud,
  And with thee refuge find;
Again let joy illume thy face,
And banish grief's desponding trace.

Thou hast the gift within thyself
  To bless thy peaceful hearth,
For can the glare of worldly pelf
  Enhance thy real worth;
Thy many virtues far outshine
The glittering lure that once was thine.

Salem, Mass., 1834.

A Sister's Lament.

I love, when evening shades the light,
To give full scope to memory's flight —
From present cares my thoughts to free,
And come o'er time and space to thee —
To where, beneath the dark blue wave,
Thou slumberest in thy ocean-grave.
Encircled in a sea-weed shroud,
Wound round thee by th' unresting flood,
Thy corpse in watery depths is laid,
    'Mid gorgeous gems whose radiant hues
    Their lustre round thy couch diffuse;
Where nought the stillness can invade,

Save requiem of the swelling surge,
While sounding forth old ocean's dirge:
And as the finny monsters sweep
Their circuit through the liquid deep,
With slackened fin o'er thee they rest,
And scan with curious eyes their guest,
Then onward through the waters cleave,
Aud thee again all lonely leave.

Full many a heart-breathed prayer for thee,
Followed thy course upon the sea,
That thou might be, in danger's hour,
Protected by Almighty power —
That He who bids the billows roll,
Would cheer and elevate the soul,
When darkening tempests should assail,
And earthly hopes and efforts fail.
And though our prayers to save were vain,
We would not murmur nor complain,
But recognize the hand of God,
And bow beneath His chastening rod.
Of thee though we have been bereft,
Thy memory behind is left,
And will with all our pleasures blend,
A sanctifying power to lend.
At times forgetfulness may cast
Its lengthening shadows o'er the past —
At times the chill of selfishness
Its blight may on my mind impress —
May turn from thee my thoughts away,
May lead from thee my heart astray —
But soon will better feelings rise,
And win me back to kindred ties,
For never can I find another
So dear as thou, my only brother.

My brother, oft I deem thee near,
In airy presence — and I hear

At times thy gladsome voice — and greet
Thy kindly smile, with love replete;
As when thou left, I see thee now.
No trace of care on cheek or brow—
Thy buoyant step and beaming eye
Betokening healthful energy;
How little then I thought that ere
Another season should appear,
Thy bark its starting-point would find.
And thou — deep sepulchred behind !

But thou wilt not for aye remain
Engulphed within the rolling main;
For when the final summon sounds,
It will pervade earth's utmost bounds;
The sea its myriads back shall give,
Death's prisoners again will live.
My brother then, a faith sublime,
Hath taught my soul, that to a clime
Exempted from the ills of this,
The pure in heart shall rise to bliss.
Like the heavenly pillars to those of old,
This hope my spirit will uphold,
And every anxious doubt repress,
While wandering through life's wilderness.

Salem, Mass., 1834.

Love's Rhapsody.

" Can I not find one friend — one faithful friend -- in whom to repose
my confidence, with whom to share my joy; I ask no more, and life has
no trial which I will not endure. The world is wide — nature is boundless
-- is there not such in existence." — *Extract*.

Such are the questionings which rise
    To agitate the youthful breast,
Nor cease until with fancy's guise
    Some fairy image hath been drest.

Some form of beauty's rarest birth,
And kindly feelings, modest worth,
Whose glance the inmost soul can thrill,
And reign supremely o'er the will,
Whose voice more musical appears
Than other tones which greet our ears,
One whom propitious heaven supplies
To make our lot a paradise.
Such hast thou ever been to me;
   A being of unworldliness —
An object of idolatry,
   Whose faintest smile had power to bless;
I have seen those more fair than thou —
   Who were more brightly beautiful,
Who could awhile around them throw
   A deeper spirit-stirring spell;
But they were all an outward glare,
And though at first they could ensnare,
And for awhile their charms endure,
Yet they could not the heart secure;
For soon unfelt is the control
Beauty alone has o'er the soul.
And they had no abiding stay,
They passed from every thought away,
To leave again a vacancy
   For other transitory things,
As evanescent as the ray
   A sunbeam on an atom flings.

But thou hast stamped a deep impress
That will defy forgetfulness,
Hath waked within my breast a strain
Whose music ever will remain;
Of all the past has given to me,
There's nought so sweet to memory
As those bright hours enjoyed with thee.

Too soon, alas, these dreams must fade
The parting hour so long delayed,
That Hope her baseless dome might rear,
Inevitably hastens near;
For there exists, I know too well,
A gulf between impassable,
And 'tis the hard decree of fate
That henceforth we must separate.

Well, I can now more calmly dwell
Upon the sadness of farewell;
A secret talisman I bear
To check the rising of despair;
The thought that thou wilt bear my grief,
Though selfishness, will give relief,
And grief divided with thy heart
Is better far than joy apart.

Salem, Mass., 1834.

The Invalid.

She moves with an agile step along,
  Arresting every eye,
The cynosure of a beautiful throng,
  Beyond all rivalry ;
The rose of health on a cheek now blooms,
  By dimpling smiles imprest,
And the spirit of joy a breast illumes,
  Where grief was rare a guest.
From the past she has gathered but delight,
  Hope's beams o'er the present play,
And visions of bliss are dancing bright
  O'er the future's flower-clad way.

There comes a change.   Disease hath paled
  Life's healthful coloring,

And the lustre of her eye is veiled
   By the shadow of death's wing ;
The voice, whose silver tones so late,
   Like song of the spring-time bird,
Could every listener captivate,
   Is now but faintly heard.
She knows the cords that bind her soul
   Within its cell of clay,
And keep it from its destined goal,
   Are slowly giving way ;
That the things of time are waxing dim,
   A mist is shrouding earth,
And her spirit must soon return to Him
   From whom it had its birth.

But though her breast with frequent sighs
   May heave regretfully,
As scenes of former revelries
   Come back to memory,
'Tis not that she would now recall,
   And live them o'er again,
But grief, that she should stake her all
   On joys so frail and vain ;
For she hath proved they cannot cheer
   Our being's parting hour,
Or deck the darkness of our bier
   With one immortal flower.
Religion now hath o'er her cast
   The gleams of its sacred joys,
And she turneth gladly from the past,
   To list to its angel voice ;
It gently o'er her soul had breathed
   A peace it ne'er had known,
And her pallid brow will soon be wreathed
   With an everlasting crown.

Salem, Mass., 1834.

11

Kindness.

"It is in vain that we would coldly gaze on such as smile upon us;
the heart must leap kindly back to kindness." — *Byron*.

Yes, such is the supreme control
Of kindness o'er the human soul ;
The feelings in their harshest mood
It softens into gratitude,
Subduing by its winning power
The evil thoughts that darkly lower,
When injuries the heart depress,
Or anger stirs to bitterness.

When by the spell of sickness bound,
The hours pass their unvarying round
Of suffering — oh, then how sweet,
The tones of those we love to greet ;
Their melody a charm conveys
To lighten up the languid gaze,
Pain's restless throbbings to allay,
And drive depression from its prey.

When bowed beneath the stern decree
Of sorrow or adversity,
The stricken one despairing droops
O'er ruined schemes and blighted hopes,
This heaven-blessed power new life can give,
The sinking energies revive,
The wounded feelings gently soothe,
Misfortune's rugged pathway smooth,
And bid again the rescued one
His onward race rejoicing run.

Enter the captive's gloomy cell,
And witness there its potent spell;
The heart that would unmoved remain,
Though lost to hope, though pierced by pain,

Though death should undisguised draw near,
And in its sternest form appear,
Will bow submissive to such sway,
And child-like weep its woes away.

The sanguinary savage yields
Free homage to the force it wields;
A trifling benefit secures
A friend in him while life endures.
It is the universal key
Which turns with ease humanity,
And strikes a chord that will resound
In every clime where man is found.

Salem, Mass., 1834.

To a Sorrowing Friend.

In any form, come when it will,
Death must some heart with sorrow fill,
Dissever from it some fond tie
Whose loss no other can supply.
It matters not, though he should find
A victim to his stroke resigned,
Hailing the summons with delight
To wing from earthly bounds his flight,
Or one who almost leaves with strife —
Convulsive clinging unto life —
Whether a friend mature in years,
In his dark kingdom disappears,
Or infancy its eyelids close,
To sink into the last repose,—
Still in some struck and quivering heart
Is felt the ruthless tyrant's dart.

And thou, my friend, hast seen the earth
Close over her who gave thee birth —
Hast heard "dust unto dust" o'er one
For whom thou gladly wouldst have gone

From all life's pleasant scenes, to rest
Within earth's all-absorbing breast.
I knew her worth — the power to move
All hearts to reverence and love
Was hers; she was too pure, I deemed,
To sojourn long on earth; she seemed
A spirit placed by some mistake
   Amid the things existing here,
That would too soon this realm forsake
   And seek again its natal sphere.
Her image is inwoven with
The memory of the past, like wreath
Of fadeless flowers, whose beauty rare
Nor time nor change can e'er impair.

Over the distance unto thee,
I send the voice of sympathy;
By a mysterious providence
Thy mother hath been taken hence,
And thou art left to find thy way
Alone, o'er life's tempestuous sea,
At early age, when most the soul
Requires her love-inspired control,
When our affections all entwine
Round her like tendrils round the vine.

But though misfortunes overwhelm,
An unseen Pilot guides the helm,
And when the friends we long have loved
Are from their wonted haunts removed,
'Tis for the best, we should believe,
For those who go and those who grieve,
And 'tis mistaken love that would
Recall again to earth the good.

Thy mother still will o'er thee bend,
Nor less than when on earth befriend;

Oft dwelling on her, you will feel
A holy pleasure o'er you steal;
She to her earthly loves will come,
To lure them to her happy home,
To loose from them the fetterings
Which earth around the spirit flings,
And animate and nerve them on,
Till they, like her, the race have won.

Salem, Mass., 1834.

Home Longings.

I saw the moisture in her eye,
And heard a half-suppressed sigh;
Fast as she brushed away a tear,
Another tell-tale would appear,
Till with averted face she strove
To hide what she could not remove,
And keep (ah vain attempt) unknown,
The grief she was ashamed to own.
I could not be at loss to know
Why sadness darkened lip and brow,
For young experience taught me why,
Were mingled thus the tear and sigh;
Such sorrowing I knew must come
From one who fondly yearned for home.

We yearn for home; we turn away
From all that would invite our stay,
And send fond memory o'er the space,
To where we left our kindred race;
'Tis there our first impressions meet
And form associations sweet,
There all our best affections find
Supports round which they freely wind,
To those we in return can give
The kindness we from them receive,

And there, perchance, the grass may wave
O'er some departed dear one's grave.

We yearn for home; through winter's time
The birds must seek a milder clime;
But when the snow-clad season yields
To spring's gay flowers and verdant fields,
On eager wings they cleave the air,
Unto their former haunts repair,
And, nest renewed, the old one near,
Their callow brood again they rear.
And when compelled by adverse fate,
From those we love to separate,
We wander forth, but never find
A home like that we leave behind.
Though for a season friendship's smile
Our homeward longings may beguile,
Or pleasure lure with its caress
The memory to forgetfulness,
Yet there are moments when we feel
Home recollections o'er us steal,
Which bid all other thoughts begone,
And occupy the mind alone;
The chords of kindred love they sweep,
  And make us wish that like the race,
Who wander through the upper deep,
  We could our journeyings retrace.

We yearn for home but when the hand
Of death has thinned its little band,
And naught meets the inquiring eye
But cold and silent vacancy,
Where once a smiling group was seen,
And all was happiness serene,
Then home no longer can impart
Its wonted joyaunce to the heart,

Nor chance nor change again restore
The charms which it possessed before;
Then from all earth can give we turn.
And for their heavenly mansion yearn.

Quincy, Mass., 1835.

————

To ———.

'Tis withered now — thy rich bouquet —
  Its life and beauty gone;
But though its bloom hath passed away.
  'Tis still a treasured boon;
The far domain from whence it came
  I never loved as yet,
Yet there are those who have a claim
  My heart can ne'er forget;

Whose fond remembrance 'mid the press
  Of constant, daily care,
Can dissipate my weariness,
  Or give me strength to bear;
Thy token bids the present flee,
  And brings them to my mind,
A talisman to memory,
  A thing with home entwined.

It speaks to me of thee, my friend —
  As bloomed these fragrant flowers,
When I received them from thy hand,
  So bloom thy youthful hours;
As in their freshness fair were these,
  So nature lavishly
Hath given thee, with a mind to please,
  The gift to charm the eye.

Like earth's fair flowers, we are taught
  That we must know decay,

The most secure in health are not
    Less perishing than they;
A truth that's traced in bold relief
    On every daily page,
A warning to the soul how brief
    Its earthly heritage.

Yet such reflections will impart
    But gloom unto the mind,
If th' pearl of priceless wealth, the heart
    As yet hath failed to find;
'Tis this, when earthly comforts fail,
    The spirit can control,
Lifting it o'er life's narrow pale
    Unto an heavenly goal.

Salem, Mass., 1834.

Striving to Unveil the Future.

Vain curiosity ! thy power
First banished peace from Eden's bower,
And drove its happy tenants forth
To toil and sweat where all was dearth.
How oft impatiently we burn
Futurity's veiled leaf to turn,
Foregoing much of present bliss
For some imagined happiness,
Or with a self-tormenting will
Forefashioning uncertain ill;
Yet could we rend the veil aside,
    Which shrouds with its mysterious folds
What is to human ken denied,
    Would what Futurity unfolds
Of all that we must bear and do,
Cause sweet contentment to ensue.

In olden times a race we find,
Endowed with more than mortal mind,
Who could intelligibly read
What the Almighty had decreed ;
Yet, who the Prophet's gift would ask,
If doomed to their unthankful task !
Driven forth into the wilderness
By those whom they had sought to bless,
And by Jehovah's stern rebuke
Again to duty driven back —
As it was with the Tishbite seer —
" *What doest thou, Elijah, here?* "

And he, the "man of sorrows," too —
　His prescience was the fruitful source,
From whence those sad reflections grew,
　Which darkened o'er His earthly course;
While duty bade Him to condemn,
He mourned o'er lost Jerusalem;
It need must be a prophet's tomb
　Should lie without the city's gate,
And truly did the Saviour's doom
　Bear witness of the prophet's fate.

Danbury, Conn., 1837.

Love's Astrology.

Among the superstitions of the French peasantry, it is mentioned by some author, that if a star shoot while a lover, who has not " passed the Rubicon," is gazing at it and thinking of his mistress, it is an auspicious omen, and denotes the successful termination of his suit.

How beautiful ye are,
　Ye orbs of silvery light —
How more than earthly fair
　To our admiring sight;
Omnipotence and love
　Hath spread ye thus abroad,

That all who look above
  May know there is a God.

The weary world around
  Is wrapt in tranquil sleep,
And not a single sound
  Breaks o'er the silence deep,
Save the discordant notes
  Of insect minstrelsy,
Or the soft breeze that floats
  In gentle murmurs by.

And at this lonely hour,
  When stillness broods o'er all,
I feel within a power
  That bids me on thee call ;
By mystic lore of earth,
  Of thee 'twas taught of old,
The events of human birth
  Thy influence controlled.

Then list ye to my plea,
  Ye luminaries fair,
Reveal the mystery —
  A lover lifts his prayer :
A form of queenly grace,
  My plaint to thee hath moved,
Of thine own loveliness —
  One who but seen is loved.

I question thee of her —
  Say, what canst thou reveal
To Love's astrologer,
  To make or mar his weal;
Thy answer I await —
  Will our existence be
Linked to a common fate
  Throughout eternity ?

Or, parted, are we doomed
  Life's scenes to wander o'er —
Our hearts to each entombed —
  Our hands to clasp no more?
Mute are ye all? — ah, no!
  Hope beams into my breast —
You augury I know —
  Your suppliant now is blest.
Danbury, Conn., 1837.

Woman at the Bed of Sickness.

He cannot linger with them long,
  Though hope the thought repel —
That pallid cheek and wasted frame
  An early death foretell;
The "hollow pageantries" of earth
  Are fading from his view,
A few more weary hours, and then
  He bids the world adieu.

A youthful form is by his couch,
  With constant watching pale —
Unasked supplying every want,
  With gentle smiles, that veil
A heart with dark forebodings filled,
  Those auguries of gloom,
Which come affection's eye to dim
  With visions of the tomb.

Before her bowed by fell disease
  An only brother droops,
Unconscious, in his feverish sleep,
  Who o'er him kindly stoops;
But as she wipes his moistened brow,
  He wakens from his dream,
And in a tone of helplessness,
  Faint murmurs forth her name.

That word — O, how the hollow tones'
　　Have moved and thrilled her breast,
Forcing from grief's deep fountain tears,
　　That will not be repressed :
It told how much was felt the love,
　　Which knew no ebbing tide,
And strove beneath a placid look,
　　Deep weariness to hide.

O, not amid the gaudy throng
　　Who wait on pleasure's shrine,
Not in the revel or the song
　　Seems Woman most divine ;
But when she bends at suffering's call,
　　To soothe its darksome hour,
Ah, then her spirit is imbued
　　With an angelic power.

And that young maiden —though her lot
　　Is with earth's toiling race —
Though Nature hath to her denied
　　The charms of form or face —
Looked lovelier in her humble sphere
　　Of patient watchfulness,
Than if enthroned as beauty's queen,
　　And robed in jewelled dress.

Danbury, Conn., 1837.

Lines Written in my Cousin's Album.

Nellie, my youthful friend, may you,
　　As on you tread life's changing way,
Find ever friends, both warm and true,
　　And strength for each succeeding day.

Life has its mission for us all —
　　To bear and do, to trust and hope —

On each will trials sometimes fall,
   With which our hearts must bravely cope.

Be yours the lot to gather flowers
   That sweetest on life's pathway glow,
And yours to find life's fleeting hours
   To years of peace and profit grow.

Waterbury, Conn., 1866.

Saddened Life.

——— "in a moment we may plunge our years
In fatal penitence, and in the blight
Of our own soul, turn all our blood to tears."—*Byron.*

They come with slow and solemn tread —
They come to sepulchre the dead,
The last sad rites of love to pay
Unto the soul-forsaken clay;
To pass through that dark scene of earth,
Which none escape of mortal birth,
When from affection's heart is wrung,
The keenest pang life's store among.

Life's lamp is quenched at early noon,
But who will say it was too soon?
When all that sweetens it has fled,
Why sorrow o'er the earth-piled bed?
O, who would call the sleeper back,
To writhe again on sorrow's rack,
Till madness came at mercy's beck, .
To hide from him his offspring's wreck.

A youthful form — her only son —
A widowed mother leans upon:
I knew him in my early days —
A comrade oft in boyhood plays;
    12

And as I trace time's backward stream,
The intervening moments seem
But as a year-encircled space,
Since last we joined the schoolboy race.

How changed, alas, his prospects now !
The brand of guilt is on his brow,
And even at his father's grave,
The jailer's presence he must brave.
That mother now is doubly lone,
Bereft at once of husband, son,
And in her hour of greatest need,
She leans upon a broken reed;
Lent by stern justice for a space
   To guide her steps unto the tomb,
To see the grave his sire embrace,
   And then reclaimed to wait his doom.

And she — the fair young flower — his wife,
How bitter is her bosom's strife !
Is it the dread Destroyer's hand
Hath touched her heart with sorrow's wand,
Causing the fearful agony
That speaks in each convulsive sigh ?
Ah, no ! the dead she cannot weep,
His slumber now is sweet and deep;
Those tear-drops gush for one whose doom
Through life is to a living tomb —
Who dead to her, though still in life,
Must leave her soon a widowed wife.

And that young cherub on her breast,
Sweet nestling in a quiet rest —
Left while in life's infantile stage
To more than orphan heritage,
Within a world each day beset,
By sin, temptation and regret,

Where error oft wears pleasure's guise,
And duty asks a sacrifice:
O'er him with fond solicitude,
Who'll watch as that lost guardian should,
For virtue's seed his mind prepare,
And from it root the early tare?

Yet deem not *he* hath turned to tears
The hopes of all his future years,
Or cursed himself throughout all time,
By long premeditated crime;
Ah, no — how oft a moment's wrong,
Reproaches keen through years prolong !
The quick revenge — the moment's hate —
Hath wrought his ignominious fate,
And given unto the blush of shame,
What else had been an honest fame.

Danbury, Conn., 1835.

Lines on a Recent Death.

Of those whose bark adown life's stream,
    Abreast of ours doth glide,
Are some, whose friendship and esteem
    May be a source of pride;
Whose kindly tones with magic skill
    Can touch the secret chords
Within the breast, which never thrill
    At the mere *sound* of words.

Such was our friend, the world among;
    We search the past in vain,
To find where envy's poisoned tongue,
    Or malice, left their stain;
A breast with generous impulse rife,
    Alive to others' woes —
His was the calm decline of life,
    Unshadowed at its close.

Yes — he was one whose earthly course
  In lines of light we trace —
Who won respect by virtue's force,
  By peaceful, pleasant ways.
With powers adapted earth to bless,
  Mysterious is the doom
Which takes him from his usefulness,
  To fill an early tomb.

He's passed into the marble sleep
  Appointed once for all,
And sorrowing age and childhood weep
  O'er his untimely fall;
Yet Faith, angelic Faith, upbuoys
  The hearts by sadness riven,
And bids them trust he now enjoys
  The unfading bliss of heaven.

He's gone! Yet none who knew him here
  Will soon forget his worth —
For much he left us to revere,
  Sojourning while on earth:
He's gone! But memory will retain,
  Within her sacred trust,
A sweet remembrance of him, when
  Dust hath returned to dust.

Danbury, Conn., 1835.

Hours of Illness.

Hushed into midnight silence deep,
  All Nature courts repose —
The worn and weary ones in sleep
  Their heavy eyelids close;
While I, within the prison walls
  Of tyrant Pain fast bound,
Have heard, at lagging intervals,
  The clock bell go its round.

Yet not without a sweet relief,
  Night's wakeful hours have passed —
Making each painful throb more brief,
  Less piercing than the last:
The trusting Faith that looks above,
  The Almighty's will to learn,
The soul's sure strengthener will prove,
  When fails the fleshly urn.

A star, by morning's light impearled,
  Bright 'mong the astral spheres,
I've watched, until a spirit's world,
  To fancy it appears.
Anon, a darksome cloud doth pass,
  Obscuring all its light,
But soon again in loveliness
  It beams upon the sight.

Thus, Heavenly Father! dost thou throw,
  Athwart our earthly light,
The chequering shades of joy and woe,
  Until life's closing night ;
But though the heart at times must droop,
  By sorrow overcast,
Thanks, Father ! for the blessed hope —
  All will be light at last !

Danbury, Conn., 1835.

———

The Drunkard's Betrothed.

The wish is vain — thou wilt not see
  The tempest gathering o'er thy way,
Nor shun the coming misery
  Which friendly eyes with grief survey.

Thou wilt not rend the veil aside
    Which passion hangs around its shrine,
Whose folds all imperfections hide,
    Nor let the light of reason shine.

Thou'rt slumbering o'er a precipice
    In willing ignorance of thy fate,
Enjoying dreams of future bliss
    From which thou'lt wake to truth — too late!

Thy blinded love's deep tenderness,
    Its idol's faith doth fondly trust ;
Clothes all his faults in virtue's dress,
    Nor thinks he e'er can be unjust.

O, burst these fetters, fraught with woe,
    Although it fill with grief thy heart;
Break from love's fatal thraldom, though
    Thy life-strings may entwine its dart.

Give not so thoughtlessly away
    The keeping of thy happiness —
He never will thy love repay,
    Nor deign thy willing smiles to bless.

It is not yet too late to heed
    Thy friends, who hold so dear thy life —
O, lean not on a broken reed,
    Do not become a drunkard's wife !

Salem, Mass., 1834.

Unforgotten.

(On the death of My daughter Katie.)

Two circles have passed of the seasons away,
Since we laid thee, dear Katie, in life's early day,
To rest on the hillside, while sun's fading rays,
And the zephyrs of evening fell soft o'er the place.

Yet still unforgotten, thy presence returns,
And the heart for lost treasure unfaltering yearns,
As at dawn or at eve, in the hours of repose,
The current of memory back to thee flows.

Thy wan hands enfolded again in our own,
As, cheek unto cheek, cometh back each low tone,
While thy glorified spirit, illumed from on high,
Uttered sweetly its parting, "Dear Mother, Good-bye!"

O fair were thy footsteps in life's busy way,
A charm in our home, as thy heart in its play
Went out in its fervor and truth toward all —
A magnet whose power we delight to recall.

Not voiceless, dear Katie, though slumbering where
The rose gives its odor to soft summer air,
And soon, as the morning's first radiance breaks,
The robin's sweet anthem in worship awakes.

Not voiceless — for echoing back through the years,
Some fond tone is stirring the fountain of tears,
While a spirit-world power lays its wand on our sight,
As we gather again in the day's fading light.

O glorified spirit! your mission to earth,
From the Fount of all good has its sanctified birth,
For ye lift the dark cloud of bereavement, and still,
With thy blest inspirations, the murmuring will.

We mourn over losses in Life's golden chain,
Yet, renewed, 'twill never be severed again,
And not until Death has ensealed loving eyes,
Can the soul, in its fulness, the Better Land prize.

Poughkeepsie, July 11, 1867.

In Memoriam.

(On the death of my daughter Hattie.)

On a fair day of June we laid her to rest,
    And the beautiful flowers that she loved so dear,
Loving hands in tenderness laid on her breast —
    Their mission of grace, like her own, ended here

The features, so rigid and wan, now no more,
    In their placid and peaceful repose,
The feverish flush and the weariness wore,
    Of the life we had watched to its close.

The imprint of Death rested pale on her brow,
    Away from the scenes to her memory dear,
But ardent home-longings, unfilled here below,
    Fruition shall know in a happier sphere.

We miss thee at morn, when the gathering comes
    From the slumberous realm of the curtained night,
We miss thee at evening, when twilight resumes
    Its spell o'er the heart in the vanishing light.

We shall miss thee, beloved, from the circles of home,
    Thy daily communings, thy part of our lives,
But tender and fresh through the years will become,
    The memories sweet of all that survives.

We lay thee to rest, to the " rest that remains,"
    By promise divine to the children of earth,
Till the cycle appointed, when angelic strains
    Shall summon the faithful to share the new birth.

Poughkeepsie, August 1, 1884.

Restoration.

(Lines written on the death of my granddaughter.)

Bright she beamed upon our vision,
　Little Hattie — star-eyed flower —
Treasure sent from fields elysian,
　Joy of life and priceless dower.

Day by day she grew in beauty,
　Cherished by parental care,
Finding pleasure in each duty,
　Building hopes on silent prayer.

There was music in the chatter
　Of her charming baby talk —
Music in the trial patter
　Of the little feet to walk.

So she grew upon our clinging,
　As of one to life as dear,
Little dreaming she was winging
　Early to her kindred sphere.

Sharp and bitter was the trial,
　To each aching, anguished heart,
As we watched, upon the dial,
　Time and Hope alike depart.

In the gloom of a great sorrow,
　Wait we darling in our pain,
Till will come the glad to-morrow,
　We shall clasp our lost again.

Rest thee in thy peaceful slumber,
　Blossom of a few brief days,
Till the years in rounded number,
　Give thee back to our embrace.

Over us in spirit hover,
　Glorified and spotless one,
That God's lessons may uncover
　Light and Hope through His dear Son.

Albany, Dec., 1885.

Sad Fatality.

While a large concourse of our citizens was at the Upper Landing on Monday evening, to witness the departure of the volunteers on the steamer *Republic*, a blast was fired, at the Ferry Dock, but a few paces distant, which sent up a number of fragments of the rock. One of them struck just below the temple of Miss Mary Southwick, daughter of Wm. C. Southwick, with a fatal shock. She was exemplary in all the walks of life, and endeared to all who were associated with her.

In a pleasant home there is gloom to-day,
For a loved and loving one passed away,
A spirit has passed from this world of ours,
And wended its way to unfading bowers.

O weep not bereaved ones, that stilly and cold,
Ye have laid her to sleep in the shroud's pure fold,
'Tis a beautiful rest 'neath the verdant sod,
For it opens a path to the garden of God.

She has left us, and Death has broken in twain,
A heart-welded link in love's kindred chain ;
But mourn for her not, for the beautiful gem
More brightly will sparkle in heaven's diadem.

Then make her a grave, where the sunbeams play
With the waving grass, through the livelong day,
Where the bright streams flow, and the glad birds sing
And the wild flowers bloom in the opening spring.

For kindred to all that is gentle and fair,
In fragrance and beauty of field and of air,
She will come in the hush of the twilight hours,
Unchanged to the vision, as fresh opening flowers.

And they bear a sweet hope in their pleasant bloom,
Of the home we must gain through the sunless tomb,
Of a peaceful existence beyond the dark grave,
Among the ransomed by Him who died to save.

Poughkeepsie, 1864.

CARRIERS'
NEW YEAR'S ADDRESSES.

WRITTEN FOR MY JOURNAL AT POUGHKEEPSIE.

1854.

Another circle of Old Time,
  Kind patrons, over us hath sped —
Again I weave my homespun rhyme,
(Perhaps you'll think it worth a dime)
  While through the Past we tread :
Though all unskilled may be my verse,
Permit me briefly to rehearse
  Events both old and new —
To lift the curtain's drooping fold,
And bid Reflection calmly hold
  Its mirror to our view;
Perhaps we thus to Faith may give
New strength a truer life to live —
  To Hope a ray impart —
Gather from Wisdom's fountain deep,
Some pearl of precious price to keep,
  An amulet for the heart —
That Love, with more unselfish aim,
May kindle up a generous flame
  For all of human mould,
In humble trust on Him who came
To cleanse our race from sin and shame,
  And draw us to His fold —
Ordaining that our love be moved
Toward Him, because "He first hath loved."

Another year! how many links
    Around the heart its record flings !
How fondly eager Memory drinks
    From all its various tinctured springs !
Love, with its golden zone, hath bound
    In happy bondage trusting souls,
And precious barques, hope-laden crowned
    With prosperous gales, o'er threatening shoals.

Time's shadow o'er the dial moves,
    And other scenes uprise to view —
Of parted friends, and household-loves,
    Companions ever dear and true;
While thus, in Retrospection warm,
    On Memory's wings we pensive turn,
We keenly feel that " Partings form
    A lesson truly hard to learn."

Death's bitter potion some have drunk —
    For who may 'scape the tyrant's stroke —
Or here, or there, some form hath sunk,
    And close entwining tendrils broke;
But while they tread this " vale of tears,"
    Their cherished hopes by anguish riven,
The mourner, upward listening hears —
    "Thy woe can find a balm in heaven."

Pause we in contemplation now to tread
The rural precincts sacred to the dead;
A Place of Rest — a picturesque retreat,
To draw from busy life our willing feet.
In quiet beauty, Nature's imprint here,
Through each revolving Season, will appear,
And Art erect, 'neath fond affection's eye,
The sculptured stone, to point where loved ones lie;
The plastic earth will own the moulder's power,
Yielding the blossoming bough and fragrant flower,

Not many changing seasons ere the soil
Yet scarcely riven by the Sexton's toil,
Will, of the Dead, a teeming mart become,
Nor heedless footsteps longer o'er it roam.
Yes, Death insatiate will his harvest reap,
For all must pass into the marble sleep:
The busy throng, elate with gainful schemes,
And Youth who build their castles high on dreams —
The Maiden, beautiful in Life's bright morn —
Old Age and Infancy — be hither borne.
Not lost this teaching, if we rightly trace,
The truth divine, to " number well our days,"
For oft, 'mid trials stern, the wayward heart
Turns from the wrong, to learn the " better part."

Our country ! How with swelling pride
  We turn to speak of thy fair fame —
How from deep fountains, gush the tide
  Of throbbing pulses — for thy aim
Is traced upon historic page
  A lesson to the tyrant throng,
Whose course is tracked, in every age,
  By deeds of robbery and wrong.
For thee, from Europe's down-crushed sons
  Go up the words of grateful prayer,
And patriots, in derisive tones,
  To meet Oppression's edicts dare.

Earth's truest noblemen here come
  A shelter 'neath thy flag to find,
To seek in Freedom's laud a home
  Where royal shackles cannot bind;
Here MEAGHER, MITCHELL, now as free
  As the proud eagle in our sky,
Sound forth to every land and sea,
  That man's redemption draweth nigh,
  13

When Crowned heads and Cossack rule
   No more shall keep their iron sway,
But in fair Freedom's peaceful school
   The nations own a brighter day.

In Smyrna Bay brave Ingraham
   Wrote terror on the tyrant's face,
When beat to arms the roll of drum,
   And brief was Austrian time of grace;
For kidnapped in a dungeon hold
   Of Austrian brigantine, there lay
One, who could claim in accents bold,
   Protection from America!
Nor fell the truth on heedless ears —
   That gallant ship with dauntless crew,
'Gainst double force for action clears,
   And snaps the prisoner's bonds in two.

Athwart old ocean's billowy way
   Is flashing fierce War's lurid light,
For gather now, in fatal fray,
   The Moslem and the Muscovite;
The grasping Northmen's countless hordes
   Of easy triumphs proudly dream,
While Omar Pasha bravely fords
   The darkly rolling Danube's stream.
Heaven for the right!   Our beating hearts
   Go wildly with each Turkish blow,
And, as the sulphurous curtain parts,
   We joy to see the Cossack low;
Heaven for the right!   Let scimetar
   And cannon ball sweep back again
The broken cohorts of the Czar,
   Dismayed within his own domain.

Our task is now finished, and heartily here,
Kind patrons! we greet you, A HAPPY NEW YEAR!

Be yours the blest path whose guerdon shall prove
A sweet Retrospection at every remove,
Till the years shall be swept 'neath Oblivion's pall,
And the Age of no changes encircle us all !

1864.

Another year has set its seal
  Upon the record of our lives,
And Time's swift-turning chariot wheel,
  Knowing no pause, right onward drives.
We may not hear his cracking whip,
  Nor motion of his gliding car.
As through life's changing scenes we slip,
  And backward look on distance far;
No toll-gate stoppings on this " pike,"
  And all may ride without a " red,"
Though Time takes toll from all alike,
  He does it while he drives ahead.
Still sweeps the bloody tide of War,
Still on our Nation's flag a star
Is here and there in dark eclipse,
Whose name now falls from saddened lips,
Persisting in an evil course,
Whose end can only bring remorse,
They struggle on against all hope,
And vainly with our forces cope.

The stubborn fight 'gainst Vicksburgh walls,
Yielding at length to Union balls,
Port Hudson's memorable strife,
  Where our own boys bore manly part.
And gallant COWLES proved with his life
  How dear the Flag was to his heart —
At Gettysburgh, now wed to fame,
  Where LEE fell back with shattered ranks,

And, balked of his expected game,
    Eager to reach Potomac's banks,
Upon whose consecrated ground,
With soldiers' graves now thickly crowned,
Our own Home Regiment, side by side,
Humbled the foeman in his pride,
And bore the stars and stripes where Death
Was treading out the warrior's breath —
On Chattanooga's famous field —
    Where Chickamaugua held its sway —
On Lookout where the foemen reeled
    Backward in panic from the fray —
All these and more of red fields won
By Union arms, and bravely done,
On SIXTY-THREE a record trace
Of valor, Time can ne'er efface.

But not upon the land alone,
The trophies of our Flag are shown ;
Our iron-clads amid the roar
Of Sumter's guns on Charleston's shore,
At shortest range their mark have made,
    Where crumbling walls and silenced gun,
And treason's flag no more displayed,
    Show that their work is well begun.
Should British Lion or Gallic Cock
    Attempt with us to interfere,
Our iron-clads will prove a shock,
    For which they 'll have a wholesome fear.
In time of peace prepare for war,
    Is an old adage, held as sound —
As pledge of peace each Monitor
    Another surety will be found.
No foreign power into this fight
    Must enter with a hostile gun,
What 'twixt ourselves we cannot right,
    'Twere better far to leave undone.

Europe now hears the alarum peal
　Of nations gathering to a fight,
Where right is shaped by ball and steel,
　And means surrendering to might.
The Corsican's successor tries
　The role his uncle tried before,
Let him keep well in mind — if wise —
　The Eagle cannot always soar.
Soon may the clouds of War disperse,
　And Peace once more our land illume,
Soon cease the desolating curse
　Which shrouds our country now in gloom ;
Soon in a Union true and strong
　May every State its safety find,
And our grand Constitution long
　In concord every section bind.

A Happy New Year ! once again,
　Kind patrons, whom we seek to please,
And as the seasons wax and wane,
　Be yours, enjoyment, health and ease.
The PRESS in daily rounds we bring,
　With gathered news from every source,
In Summer, Autumn, Winter, Spring,
　All times, all seasons, in their course ;
A welcome may it find from you —
　So will our labors lightened be,
Whether the year be old or new,
　Thanks for that *postal currency.*

1865.

Our greeting, kind patrons, again we renew,
As thoughtful we say to the Old Year adieu,
And welcome with hope the dawn of the New.
The New Year has brought us again to your door

To talk o'er events which have marked '64;
With our carrier's address we wait on you here
And wish you sincerely a Happy New Year.

What change has been wrought in the year now gone by,
To quicken the heart and to moisten the eye?
How many fair prospects which welcomed its birth,
Have failed in their pride and are lost upon earth,
How many have left us whose lines are now set,
Where sentinels challenge with sharp bayonet,
Each moment exposed to the rallying call
Which ushers them on to the steel or the ball,
Or, on the wide ocean, or gun-shotted deck,
Watch day and by night rebel rovers to check,
All patient awaiting the hour of release,
When grim-visaged War shall surrender to Peace,
And freed from privations of camp and of field,
Return to the pleasures that happy homes yield,

Well, what of Eighteen Sixty-four,
As brief we trace its record o'er —
What has it done to link to fame
By great and lasting deeds its name?

Abroad, the men who rule at will,
Have set two people on to kill;
The Holsteiner and Dane have fought,
Yet who can tell what good it brought?
Somebody pays a round war tax,
For Louis Nap. to grind his axe.

In Mexico they've flopped about,
And Maximilian now they shout;
There Santa Anna had his day,
And Miramon and Juarez;
Their presidents are obsolete,
Crushed out beneath imperial feet.

What of the night at home? How goes
The battle with our stubborn foes?
The year's experience opes a page
Which will go down to after age,
And wondering they'll ponder o'er
The great events of Sixty-four.

Ho! for the Wilderness! and Grant
Flung out his banner, "en avant!"
'Twere long to tell of that dread fray,
  Where hand to hand the foemen stood,
No charging columns in array,
  But ball and bayonet in the wood;
A dense and darkened atmosphere,
  Where foes upspringing to the strife,
Out of the darkness would appear,
  And fought lone-handed, life for life.
Long was the fight. The scythe of Death
  Swept fearful through that gallant band,
And many a brave soul fell beneath
  The star-gem'd banner of his land;
But victory crowned the patient deeds
  Of men resolved to win or fall.
And Richmond saw our prancing steeds
  And serried ranks before her wall.

In Shenandoah valley, where
  The varying contests foes had waged,
Braving the rebel in his lair,
  Phil. Sheridan the foe engaged;
Linked to historic fame, that vale
  Will furnish long the thrilling tale,
Of war's great sacrifices made,
And life on patriot altar laid.

Atlanta held defiant sway,
  A boasted rebel entrepot,

Till Sherman turned his guns that way,
 And soon his pride was humbled low.
Onward they moved, a chosen few,
Keeping unchecked their end in view,
Till on Savannah's lofty towers,
The stars and stripes proclaimed it ours.

Vain Hood on Nashville laid his eyes,
Resolved to capture by surprise;
Thomas would not be " Hood-winked " so,
But gave him a " ticket-of-leave " to go —
And go he did with guns behind,
No longer for the fight inclined.
Bold Farragut, the brave old tar,
Who boss'd the fight, lashed to the spar,
Pluckily enters Mobile Bay,
And soon his cannon end the day,
And fort and fleet succumb, his prey.

But we no longer will rehearse
Heroic deeds in hasty verse:
We cannot paint each scene by scene
Which in the two years intervene:
Many the deeds unknown to fame,
Which gild a humble soldier's name;
Many a voice in death now still,
In hottest charge rung strong and shrill.
Would that these gory days were past,
And we had seen of War the last,
Would that the hands now closed in hate
 Again might clasp in friendly thrill,
And joined in Union, State by State,
 Fraternal laws again fulfill.

O, darkest hour of fallen earth,
When men forget the ties of birth —
When Passion's rule invokes a spell,
To make on earth another hell —

When through a blind revenge is spurned
The good our fathers dearly earned,
And Civil War, Sin's darkest child,
O'er earth's best progress riots wild.

Our song is now ended — kind patrons adieu,
We hope to our duty henceforth to be true;
We bid you good speed as you move on your way,
Your path strewed with blessings as day succeeds day,
And may a kind Providence so keep you here,
Your lives may be glorified in that blest sphere,
Where War shall no longer infuse its red leaven,
And victory mean the full triumph of Heaven.

1866

A New Year's call — we come again —
    Kind patrons of the DAILY PRESS,
And offer you in humble strain
    Our Happy New Year's brief Address;
And 'tis a Happy New Year now
    To rich and poor, to old and young,
For on our Union's arch the bow
    Of welcome Peace again is hung.

Four years of civil strife have run
    Their fearful race, baptized in blood —
How long it seems since War begun,
    And brethren first as foemen stood !
How mingled were our fears and hopes,
    Till Sherman's march dissolved the spell,
And onward passed his gallant troops —
    Till Lee gave up and Richmond fell.
Then Grant confirmed with crowning grace
    The people's trust in him reposed,
And standing in the conqueror's place,
    With generous terms the struggle closed.

Lincoln fell 'neath the assassin's stroke,
  And a whole people mourned his fate,
A deed so foul at once awoke
  In every breast a holy hate;
No grander tribute e'er was paid
Than that upon his coffin laid,
Proving, whatever may divide
The people, in their party pride,
They turn instinctive in their might,
When Wrong usurps the place of Right.

In Andrew Johnson now we hail
The patriot's hope, whate'er assail —
Though Faction lifts its hydra head,
On just and equal laws to tread,
And clamors for continuous strife,
At peril of the Nation's life,
The statesman firm of Tennessee,
In footsteps of Old Hickory,
Stands squarely by the sacred chart,
So dear to every freeman's heart —
The CONSTITUTION (grand bequest)
Which North, nor South, nor East, nor West,
Has different import to the State
Whose laws assent to its just weight.
Defender of this cause so just,
In Andy Johnson we will trust,
Hold up his hands with hopeful zeal,
Nor doubt that Time all griefs will heal.

John Bull has been our dear old friend
  " Over the left," all through this fight,
Ready his guns and ships to send,
  As " neutral " gifts with vast delight;
O, generous John; O, model court,
  Rebellion's helping call to meet,

Whose cruisers swarmed from every port,
  To burn and sink our commerce fleet.
But soft, we hear a different strain,
  As Fenian slogans ring afar,
John Bull cries loudly o'er the main,
  Alarmed at Pat's " E pluribus bragh!"

At home the " Wearing of the Green "
  Is fiercely banned by prison bars.
But Pat derides Bull's harmless spleen
  Where float aloft the stripes and stars;
He shakes his pipe at Canada,
  And Bull sends out his grenadiers,
And quaking crown and armed array
  Attest the Briton's nervous fears.
What though in Tara's Halls not now,
Shall shamrock wreathe some kingly brow,
To speak for Ireland as of yore,
When her own blood the sceptre bore —
What though divided counsels break
The link heart-forged for Erin's sake —
Yet shall perfidious Albion feel
  Forebodings of that coming day,
When Retribution's judgment peal
  Shall echo from the Thames to Tay.

Europe's crowned heads have sent us o'er
A Maximilian to this shore;
He comes equipped with crown and seal,
Bearing Nap's " recommend " in steel;
When Jonathan the order signs,
To give Max Montezuma's mines,
'Twill then be time enough to blow
Nap's empire trump in Mexico.

But let him watch his new-found clime,
For Andy only bides his time;

That time will come when banded hearts
Shall beat as one in all our marts,
And jealous of the good old rule,
Taught in our earlier statesmen's school,
Shall sweep like Marion's legions o'er,
And rout usurpers from the shore,
Where'er the people lift the cry
Of help from foreign tyranny.

Our City Home may justly claim
Some marked addition to her fame;
Since last our annual gift we bore,
VASSAR has opened wide her door,
Where woman finds on varied page
Grandest endowment of the age,
And fills, with recognition meet,
The limits of this classic seat,
Nor need there be complaint of want
Of Education's ample grant.

The kindly band of woman lifts
The cloud of want by timely gifts,
And softens rugged Winter's reign
To shivering limbs and aching frame,
Work for the strong, care for the weak,
Dark homes with healing hands they seek.

1867.

We come with our offering again at your door,
The Old Year is passed, and the New Year before
Is tracing already, in light or in shade,
On all a deep impress that never can fade.

We pause on its threshold, with feelings subdued,
As backward we glance o'er the paths we have trod ;
A sheaf has been added to memory's store,
A year has been linked with the years gone before

In the chain of our being — that mystical bond
Reaching back through all time to all time beyond,
As a parcel and part of Humanity's whole,
Where'er beats a pulse or looks upward a soul.

Each heart has its lingering places, more dear
To itself than all else, in the fast flying year ;
Each heart its own fountain of grief, welling o'er
For treasures now lost on that desolate shore ;
Its holiday promise to many has turned
A shadow of sadness for hopes darkly urned :
To mortal experience the moral is sure,
Life's cup must be mingled while Time shall endure.
Yet who from this truth, alike to all blood,
Shall murmuring turn, though not understood,
Or doubt that all trials befalling us here,
For the best, in the sight of true wisdom appear,
Where the heart to itself and to others is true,
And to each and to all gives the Golden Rule due.

The land where our pride and affection belong,
May claim for a moment the theme of our song.
It has come from the furnace of trial erect,
No stain on its banner to dim self-respect ;
There shall still be one people intact, as of yore,
For the oppressed an asylum, from whatever shore,
With equal protection — opportunity same —
Shielded each and alike, of whatever name.
What though there still linger the leaven of hate,
To keep us antagonized — state against state —
What though clashing factions, hedged fierce in the way,
A union of hands and of hearts may delay,
Yet, softened by time, shall the enmity yield,
And fountains of national discord be sealed ;
Redeemed thus, more truly than ever 'twill be,
In homage to law, the blest "land of the free."

14

Not alone on our shores has the Demon of War,
Levied hosts to the fields to be crushed by his car,
And in the red van of fierce squadrons borne down
The scepter of state and the title of crown —
Repeating the lesson oft taught us of yore,
That the test of the right is the mailed arm of power.
In the stern Prussian text of the Bonaparte creed,
The choice is a short one — "submit or you bleed!"
Whatever the cavil to work so begun,
One thing is quite certain — with promptness 'twas done,
Enforcing the maxim which sometimes is right,
"What your hands find to do, to do with your might."
Let us hope that these changes, so costly in blood,
May bring to the people a harvest of good,
Though stern be the discipline, out of the fire
Oft comes the ordeal that nations require,
To fit them to work for that era of mind,
When men shall uplift, and not drag down, their kind.

O'er the soil of our Mexican neighbor the sword
Is flashing in conflict, and cannon are heard,
Imperial armies still rule his domain,
Though met in fierce conflict on many a plain,
Where national memories kindle his zeal,
To drive back invaders at point of the steel;
Will he triumph? Who doubts, tho' long has his race
Been plundered by robbers, installed in high place,
His industry crippled — his labor a doubt —
His ruler thrown up on the last rabble's shout,
To have and to hold in his greed, because brief,
'Till the next stronger faction sets up a new chief.
Yet while bitter factions may hinder the day
When a foreign crowned prince shall forfeit his sway,
A will that is born of a nation's great need,
When struggling with foes, rarely fails to succeed.

All quiet in Ireland! so reads the report,
Of censors who speak in behalf of the court;
All quiet in Ireland! Perhaps it is so,
Fate rules that not yet is the time for the blow ;
But the muttering thunder has not been in vain,
Though dying away it may yet boom again.
Let the Rulers beware, and with equity steer,
Ere the ghost of " Boroïhme " again shall appear ;
Let them temper with mercy and more equal law,
Their national dealings with " Erin go bragh ! "

Strung through the far ocean depths, marvellous link !
Its message performed in a flash or a wink,
A lightning conductor, the two worlds between,
The CABLE its mystery works out unseen ;
Of all the world's wonders, on history's page,
This conquest will lead as the pride of the age.

We close with our errand, kind readers, once more,
Hoping still with our DAILY to call at your door ;
May the shadows of evil which fall on your way,
By true hearts be lightened and brief be their stay,
Till, past the uncertainties bounding us here,
May you find an eternally Happy New Year !

1868.

A Happy New Year! is the voice of to-day,
  Ringing cheerily out from the hurrying throng,
And joining the chorus our tribute we pay
  To all our kind patrons in annual song.
How rapid the tide of Old Time since our call,
  A twelve-month agone, was made at your door,
How the weeks and the months, from winter to fall,
  Have sped quickly on to another year's shore.

We part with the Old and we welcome the New,
  With friendly salute, and with festival cheer —

Let us pause for a moment, in rapid review
  Of events strongly marked on the fast fading year.

The nations of the Old World keep
  With little change their wonted way ;
Their " war-dogs " now, in muzzled sleep,
  No longer track through blood their prey ;
Yet, with a watchful eye, each King,
  Keeps border lookout for his foe,
Lest, like a panther's sudden spring,
  An invader strike a hostile blow.

Old Johnny Bull is in a stew,
  Bothered by Fenian buccaneers,
He hardly knows what first to do,
  So many stories reach his ears :
Now Guy Fawkes plots, all snugly laid,
  Set Johnny's eye-balls all astare —
Explosive letters next have made
  To rise, on stiffened end, his hair,
O Johnny ! there 's a lesson true,
  You should no longer disregard,
For sure it now comes home to you —
  " The way of the transgressor 's hard."

A passing cloud o'er Italy
  Awoke the breath of war to life ;
It failed — and there again we see
  An end of internecine strife.
O'er Crete's fair island Turkish wrong
  Has carried rapine, sword and fire —
The weak swept down before the strong,
  The babe, the mother and the sire.
Yet slow the tyrant's power to crush
  The patriot struggling for his home,
Though war's red flame may o'er him rush,
  He bravely stands amid the gloom ;

The stag, when brought to bay, will turn
 In furious struggle with his foe,
And this may the oppressor learn,
 Where'er he strikes a dastard blow.

O'er Mexico no longer waves
 The banner of imperial power,
For sleep they now in martial graves
 Who ruled in regal state their hour ;
The invader's foot, deep-tracked in blood,
 Is swept from Montezuma's Hall,
And where his flaunting legions stood
 Now stand the legions of the soil.
Yet waits there still the reign of law —
 For civic rights protection due —
The firmness which should overawe
 Each plunder-led guerilla crew.
Perchance e'en there shall Science, Art,
 And Labor, win enduring fame —
Commerce may find its ship-thronged mart,
 And make in fact what 's but in name.

Now homeward let us turn the eye,
 Where far Atlantic rolls its shore —
What do the year's events supply
 Of note, to swell our carrier's store.
We've stretched our borders far to north,
 Where polar bears and icebergs roam,
Seven millions plump in gold 'twas worth —
 At least we had to plank that sum.
Down where the gulf stream holds its course,
 One of West India's sea-girt isles,
Where earthquakes madly spend their force,
 St. Thomas, looks on us and smiles.
And Cuba, proud Castilia's queen.
 Is only waiting for the " rocks,"
To hand us o'er her island green —

The key which gulf-way trade unlocks.
A better way than that of old,
　　Which now your neighbor's laud secures —
When knocks were used instead of gold —
　　Harsh threats instead of "kindly yours" —
We rob nowadays in gentler style,
　　For Uncle Sam's gold box we tap,
And pick up here and there an Isle,
　　To add unto our country's map.

A " reconstruction peace " now reigns,
　　After a fashion — modern quite —
When Brother Sambo best explains
　　The plan to mix up black and white.
His genius regulates the code
　　For States once holding high renown
For legal lore of men the abode
　　Who bravely fought with Washington.
Out of the gloom let us, hopeful still,
　　Trust there will rise to save the land,
Men who nobly their places will fill,
　　And link with their efforts a patriot band.

A Happy New Year ! we will utter again,
　　To the friends who have kindly remembered our toil,
A year may it be, unshadowed with pain,
　　A year whose review shall be pleasant to all.

1869.

The rolling months have brought again
　　The season of our annual call —
We come to wish, in humble strain,
　　A Happy New Year to you all.

A Happy New Year ! how they roll !
　　These circlets of Old Father Time —
Speeding our footsteps to that goal
　　We heed but lightly in life's prime.

Farewell Old Year with locks of white,
  Your faltering steps and wrinkled brow,
And shadows deepening into night,
  The same old story tell us now.

While pausing on your utmost verge,
  Thought travels o'er your changeful way,
And Time, with muffled tongue, your dirge
  Is tolling out.   Let us list the lay: —

Old Year! have you kept the promise you made,
When, a twelvemonth since our tribute we paid
To the incoming year, with its beaming eye,
And " castles of air " adorning the sky ?

Have visions you painted in rainbow's hues
All vanished from earth like morning dews ?
Have silvery words from your flattering tongue
Died like echoes of song, on the night-air flung ?

Have hopes that you raised turned into despair,
The day-dreams of youth into anxious care ?
Have you ruthlessly crushed the drooping flower
And the bending reed, with a tyrant's power ?

Old Year! Old Year! in your casket to-day
How many rich jewels are hidden away !
And our eyes are now turned to the glory-clad shore,
Where these polished gems shall fade nevermore.

You shattered our idols and deep was the blow,
You led us in paths we were shrinking to go :
Ah ! well, if when tasting the bitterest draught,
The waters of healing they proved, as we quaffed.

For blessings and mercies renewed day by day,
For guidance and strength in a devious way,
For every good gift from a kind Father's hand,
With thankful emotions our hearts should expand.

And oh ! as the record is made up on high,
Of failures and faults in the year now gone by,
For us may some guardian angel appear,
To blot from remembrance with cancelling tear.

Farewell, dying year ! For we meet nevermore,
Your sunlight is dim on the fast fading shore;
Reviewing your path, smiles mingle with tears,
Pass on to the list of the long-vanished years.

And now with a welcome we turn to the new,
    To the hopes and the trials its coming may bring;
Whatever its pathway now hidden from view,
    May strength for the duty abundantly spring.

Sustained in high purpose to battle with Wrong,
    Inspired by the courage allied to the Right,
Let the lesson be heeded each household among —
    What our hands find to do, let us do with our might.

Our voices to-day shall be tuned to glad cheer,
    And lively emotions enkindle each heart,
For festival tokens become the New Year,
    As on its diversified journey we start.

Let us garland its hours with blossoms of hope,
    Never borrow concern over uncertain ill,
Resolved with its trials to manfully cope,
    And meet all its crosses with resolute will.

We live in an era when mind must be quick
    To meet and to master the problems of life —
When startling events are crowding us thick,
    And salient issues with conflict are rife.

Far away does the echo of turbulent sounds
    Break out 'neath the pressure of tyrannous power,
And, driving to counsel the fear-stricken crowns,
    Now burden with anxious emotions the hour.

Yet the wisdom to rule — not the patience to bear —
   Is the want of mankind, now than ever more clear;
For the ruled, let the rulers have generous care,
   And the cloud now uprising would soon disappear.

Turn homeward our glance, and our hope will not fail,
   That our nation again shall resume its high state,
When conflicts, that now its reunion assail,
   Shall yield to the spirit which conquers all hate.

When hand unto hand, and each heart unto heart,
   No longer distrusting, unfriendly will feel,
But in all our wide limits shall act the true part,
   And catch the old spirit with mutual zeal.

Our task shall now end, with a wish for you all,
   Kind patrons, whom daily our footsteps attend,
That the lines of your household, wherever they fall,
   With peace and prosperity ever may blend;

Each New Year may add to the sum of all good,
   Each trial be followed with consequent gain,
And amply with happiest blessings endued,
   We may meet you approved on a New Year again.

1870.

Another New Year now calls for our rhyme,
A year rounded by a new decade of Time;
We come with our annual song of good cheer,
Wishing each — wishing all — a Happy New Year.

The old had its mission — its good and its ill —
Its joys to enliven, its sorrows to chill;
What hopes it has withered 'tis not ours to show,
For the heart its own bitterness only can know.
Along its dim shore many a bark has gone down,
Whose sails were unfurled in a heart-lighted zone,

Rich laden with treasures no wealth could e'er buy,
And leaving a want which time ne'er can supply;
For whate'er we add to the sum of our bliss,
Can ne'er fill the void of the dear ones we miss,
And no broken tie but jars sad on the heart,
For its answering chord can no new one impart.
Yet no sky wears ever its draping of gloom,
And no waste so sterile as never to bloom;
In each rounded day, if but rightly divined,
No heart so o'er cast but some sunlight will find,
Some motive to action, new strength to sustain,
When burdens grow heavy from life's weary strain.
Thus, like summer landscape, when passing clouds play,
Do sunshine and shadow alternate our way;
Brood not o'er the problem, for wise purpose given,
'Till "the Temple of God shall be opened in heaven."

And now, o'er another year parted we stand,
Its record to note of our own native land.
Abundance has crowned the resources of earth,
And Pestilence far has been kept from the hearth;
In wide fields of labor the strong hand of toil
Has reaped its reward from the generous soil,
And not less hath the skill of the artisan,
In creative power its due recompense won;
The varied blessings, which so many miss
In less favored lands, have been poured upon this.

Change now this fair picture to matters of State,
And look o'er a land ruled by sectional hate —
The graspings of power, guided only by force —
In reaching its aims, riding rough-shod its course —
States made or unmade, as a faction may need,
Dividing, ejecting, to suit party greed;
The ermine struck downward and made to succumb
To Congressional Catalines — crouching and dumb!
Ah! well would it be, if the rulers and ruled,

In the spirit which governed our fathers were schooled;
Then again would we see in one brotherhood link,
In prosperous union, all enmities sink,
And hear the glad pæan, from shore unto shore,
"The peacemaker's mission is joyously o'er."

Unsettled and restive, across the blue main,
The masses are struggling to throw off the chain,
In the "long ago" forged, to make monarchy strong,
When peoples were taught that Kings ne'er could do wrong.
The red fields of war have not saddened the eye,
On Europe's fair plains, in the year just gone by;
But the long fretting discord goes steadily on
To a final result, between subject and crown.

The cliffs of Old England have beat back the surge,
For ages assailed by the storm's angry dirge;
But a foe more unyielding now meets the proud front
Of regal tradition, nor quails in the brunt;
'Tis the ripened conviction of resolute men,
Demanding Reform, both with bold speech and pen,
'Tis Ireland's just call, in her plundered estate,
Long slighted, yet doomed not much longer to wait,
For Ministries changed, in the war against wrong,
Betoken a time when the weak shall be strong.

France hears the loud tokens of popular hate
Of absolute sway, in her halls of debate;
In her streets, in her workshops, the leavening thought
That men should be free, is now fearlessly taught.
"The Empire is Peace," said a voice from the throne —
Where bayonets sustain it, no peace can be known;
" The Empire's concession," is the voice of to-day,
Lest palaces tremble again in the fray.

Through the sterile old wastes of the Orient realm
A channel is bearing the commerce-bound helm;

Two seas, like the Siamese Twins, are now wed,
The Mediterranean linked with the Red;
A triumph of skill — how the dark-browed Turk
Must revolve in his mind this wonderful work,
And the swart sons of Egypt, with new kindled life,
See stagnant old deserts with commerce now rife,
While harem and mosque, hear the on-coming tread
Of a power more transforming than Bonaparte led.

Ring out for poor Cuba the well-wishing strain,
Beset as she is by the minions of Spain;
In the land of George Washington hers was the right
To words of good cheer in her glorious fight —
To the moral effect of a strong-spoken word,
When the White House in message with Congress conferred.
Has she found it?   Ah, no! but been coldly repelled,
Our ship-yards her enemy's navy has swelled,
While our one-sided rulers with hostile parade,
Through vigilant spies have denied them all aid;
In time long to come will the story be told —
That Cuba had nothing — the Spaniards had gold.

From scenes far away we now turn in adieu,
Nor weary you more with our hurried review;
Let us welcome the New Year with earnest intent,
That in higher endeavor its days shall be spent,
That in all its surroundings of home, by our aid,
Each rising of strife shall be gently allayed,
Each burden divided, to lessen its weight,
Sustained by the lesson, whatever our fate,
That the noblest example on earth ever given,
Left "altars of sacrifice" nearest to heaven.
And thus will the passage of Time but unfold,
More clearly to vision, what never grows old, —
That the soul rightly kept on its mission while here,
Will find in all changes a HAPPY NEW YEAR.

1871.

We stand on the threshold of seventy-one —
How swiftly the seasons their circuit have run !
A year has been dropped in the tomb of the past,
Since your carriers called on their song-visit last —
A year, let us hope that to you has been fraught
With much more to gladden than sadden the thought.

Each year has its record unshared as its own,
As Nature and Life by their changes are known —
Some salient features of virtue or crime,
That specially mark it in eras of Time ;
And in the review of another one fled,
Our thoughts let us fix on its eventful tread.

To kingdoms and peoples, across the broad main,
The New Year has come under war's fearful strain ;
An empire has fallen — an Empire been made !
How glaring the " whirligigs of Time " are displayed !
The reign of o'erreaching ambition, uncrowned,
Was hurled in the height of its pride to the ground ;
Fair fields plowed by cannon, running over with blood,
Now show where, embattled, vast armies have stood ;
Relentless and savage, traditional hate,
By Zouave and Uhlan have worked out its fate ;
The hearth-stones of nations engaged in this strife,
Show the cost of crowned heads is the current of life,
And desolate homesteads, where want rules the day,
And mourning their lost ones, grow thick in the fray.

O, saddest of aspects, when war's brutal force,
To settle disputes, is the only recourse ;
How paltry the glory of satisfied lust,
Which rears up its idol on human hearts crushed,
When pride, through the bloody carnival of war,
Fiercely burns to extend its dominion afar.

15

How slow are the rulers of Europe to heed
The historic moral of diadem greed —
Reaching out, reaching out, with coveting hand,
And flimsiest pretext, for some neighbor's land.

Yet who shall the limits assign to events,
Or to day draw the scope of its mate a year hence?
The darkness pervading the primeval hour,
By the bursting of light was debarred of its power,
So 'neath the dark cloud where the masses now tread,
Will their gospel of higher condition be read :
Nor vainly for liberty shall they aspire,
Though their pathway lead through a baptism of fire,
Yet the sword shall be sheathed, war's terrors shall cease,
And all shall acknowledge the blessings of peace.

A beautiful island, and not far away,
Where sparklings of sunlight on ocean waves play,
Where buds of the orange, the lemon, and lime,
Are types of the beauty of soil and of clime,
By the minions of Spanish oppression beset,
Still with the life-blood of its children is wet,
While, ravaged and wasted, its once fertile fields
No longer their tribute to industry yields ;
Our neighbors they are, yet with coldness of mien,
Our rulers no comfort or aid intervene,
And while our Republican cheer they invoke,
Their pleadings pass only through vistas of — smoke !

From climes thus entrammeled by tyranny's hand,
Let us turn now with joy to our own native land,
Whose spreading domain is a heritage free
Of a people who bend to no tyrant the knee.
In the year just departed our land has been blest
In a measure that gladdens each patriot breast;
Of its fruits, let us mention, with national pride,
That State unto State has been closer allied,

That union of feeling, resuming the sway,
To closer fraternity ushers the way,
When a union of hearts with a union of hands
Shall strengthen its claim as the hope of all lands.

Nor can we, while counting the gains of the year,
Unmindful pass over its promises here —
Here to our fair city, now bound with new bands
To the people and homes which the iron now spans:
To the zeal and the enterprise, working with will
To open new channels for traffic to fill,
In the signs of home progress now meeting the eye,
New sources of comfort and health to supply,
The words of approval which fairly belong,
Let us freely accord in our carrier song.

And now to our patrons few words we address:—
Our thanks for your aid in sustaining the PRESS;
Through you it must flourish — through you must our cause
Gain converts to cherish our freedom and laws.
A new page is opening of Time, may it be,
In all its recordings to thine and to thee,
New sources of pleasure — new help from above —
To weave round its duties the garland of love,
So when it shall in its December appear,
'Twill have been to you all — A Happy New Year!

1872.

Your carrier's call for Seventy-two —
A Happy New Year this to you !
Heaven grant its daily course may be
From dark misfortune wholly free,
That gathering hope and strength, you may
Tread with light heart life's roughest way,
Filled with a sense of present good,
By each returning sun renewed.

A year dies out, and backward thought
Takes up the lessons it has taught;
And, as in shrouded state it lies.
While Nature pays 'her obsequies,
As midnight orbs look glittering down
On mantled earth with snow bestrewn,
We catch the spirit of the truth —
That Time must pass to age from youth —
That Death in his appointed hour,
Will over all assert his power —
To parting year, or loved at home.
Its summons once to all must come.

We turn to foreign lands to read
   The records of the year just passed —
Do they the lesson wisely heed
   Of bitter feuds in battle cast?
The clouds of war no longer brood
   O'er devastated fields and homes,
And peace now reigns o'er dwellings rude,
   O'er marts of trade and palace domes;
Yet lingering still, resentful fires
   Are burning 'neath their ashes gray,
While dwells the thought with sons and sires,
   Revenge but waits its ripened day;
And still does crowned exaction strip
   The masses of their daily toil,
Watching the favored hour to slip
   Their " war-dogs " on some neighbor's soil.—

Soon will the drama change — yes, soon,
   " VOX POPULI VOX DEI " be
The light of an effulgent noon
   To disenthralled humanity;
And then shall come the era new,
   When sceptered power and rights of caste

No longer shall endow the few,
  And leave the rest in bondage fast —
When greed of conquest, born of kings,
  Shall be a branded, unknown aim,
Squelched by a brotherhood which brings
  In oneness all of every name.

The Old World rests from war's alarms,
But in the New, the clash of arms
And raging factions, curse the lands
Now reddened by contending bands.
Cuba still wears a foreign yoke,
And pleading looks through battle smoke;
Her lands by ruffian hands are bared,
And neither age nor sex is spared.
Gem of the Antilles! shall the cry,
Of thy long years of agony,
Awake at last the sympathy
  Of those who struggled once like thee —
Who found at last an outstretched hand,
Reached to them from a foreign band,
Ready to help a struggling land
  Become from iron bondage free!

" Pizzaro's conquest," once begun
In Mexico, is never done;
Still schemes of conquest rule the land,
A chief in each guerilla band,
While sharp beset, poor Juarez
Is like a hunted stag at bay,
And all around, the bristling pack,
For change of rule, is on his track.

Southern Republics run to fight,
Like insects to an evening's light —
And, learning nothing, quick return,
To revel in another burn!

What burlesque this, on popular rule —
The jingling bells and cap of fool
Should hang above each chair of State,
From Mexico to Rio Le Plate!

We turn our vision homeward now —
   What of the year in our own clime,
Where proudly spans the promise bow,
   To welcome all of every clime.
With ample store has Nature's yield
Crowned labor in the harvest field;
Through all the avenues of trade
Has flowed for all substantial aid;
Much to uplift the thankful soul
   Now retrospects the thoughtful gaze,
As standing at the old year's goal
   We look back on its buried days;
No Nation blessed as ours has been,
Should fail to keep in memory green,
A conscious sense of gratitude
For vital gifts each year renewed;
Not here should base corruption show
Its baneful upas, sweeping low —
Not here should public trust be made
A gift to use in venal trade;
Where much is given, a rule inspired
Asserts, that much will be required;
If, honored thus, our Nation stands
In proud precedence of all lands,
Her beacon-lights should purely burn,
   And throw their radiance far and wide,
That others, seeing them, may learn
   Safely their storm-bound ships to guide.

A startled nation hears the cry *
As swift the fearful rumors fly,
That a great city, central mart

---

* Fire at Chicago.

Of commerce, literature and art,
Beneath a fiery deluge lay,
Helpless and crushed within a day;
While from the Northern forests came *
Tidings alike of wasting flame,
Where fellow mortals strove in vain,
From circling fire a goal to gain.—
Not narrowed down, by clime or creed,
Came noble cheer in word and deed,
For the broad heart of human kin,
These stricken ones took helping in.

Not shortened is the lofty thought,
    As taught us by the poet's line,
When thus to our conviction brought —
    Something there is in all divine;
The moral of the battle-field,
    But teaches passion's willful course,
And slight the sum of all revealed
    In public life, but selfish force;
But in this great responsive sight,
    The Golden Rule impulsive owned,
We recognize in clearer light
    A heaven-born sentiment enthroned.

Patrons, we close.   There is, 'tis said,
    " An end to all things under sun,"
And you may think our rhyming spread
    As effort past this rule to run.
As on the New Year now you tread,
    A happy season to each one,
So may you gather from its store,
    Of all that leaves a real good,
Fuller than all that years before
    Upon your onward path have strewed.

* Forest fires at Peshtigo.

1877

" How swift the seasons come and go !
These years of ours — in silent flow
Marking their coming and their flight,—
Now seen, now vanished from the sight —
The same as when, in Eden's prime,
Man first stood on the shores of Time,
Unchanged, though peoples and their place
Have vanished from the Earth's broad face —
Alike to every human heart,
Since Time unrolled its mystic chart,
Some cause to mourn, some hope to cheer,
The moral of the Opening Year.

A New Year ! and the past one old,
Its mission closed, its requiem tolled,—
The one of present use and thought,
The other ended and forgot ?
Not this the meaning of the break
Which only changing figures make;
Our life, in many a clasp, linked close,
No such division ever knows;
Treasures there are which grow not old,
And links which never lose their hold;
The patient toilers by our side,
In life's hard battles often tried,
The self-forgetful hearts that find
In others' good their own entwined,
In daily duties, trusting love,
A joy and hope all else above —
These grow not old, but brighter burn,
As Time's dividing dates return,
Nor change nor seasons ever know,
Save as they more divinely grow.

There's greeting for the New Year now —
  A timely wish, and great its need;

As breaks the sun o'er mountain brow,
  O may its gifts bring light indeed —
Light to cheer up the darkened homes,
  Where willing toil lacks answering prayer,—
Such reassuring light as comes
  After long vigils with despair;
For weary now the burden lies
  On many a hearth beneath a cloud,
Where shortened means and scant supplies,
  Make drear the time of winter's shroud.

A New Year for the Nation, too —
  A higher grade of public life —
A patriot thrill the country through,
  To cure the curse of selfish strife;
Not this the soil where perjured lust
  For power and place ignobly won —
Not here success, through venal trust,
  Should rear its head and justice shun.

And how shall poet pen unfold
  The monstrous evil of our time,
The right of suffrage swapped for gold,
  The shameless, while the deepest, crime;
This priceless boon of manhood, wrung
  From tyrant hands, beyond all cost,
To scheming knaves is idly flung,
  As worthless thing and cheaply lost.

Voices from out the past are heard,
  Rising above the Babel hue,
And as we list the pulse is stirred,
  For they who speak were tried and true ;
Tried in the furnace where the soul
  Showed the pure stamp of patriotism,
No half-heart service, but the whole,
  Above all narrow creed or schism ;

A retrospect beyond compare,
  In all that makes a nation grand —
Shall we not heed this voice afar,
  Re-echoed from a later band,
And in its patriotic strain,
  Great memories invoke once more,
The while we may renew again
  Our birthright pride, now humbled sore?

Home of our Washington! we turn
  Far back to other days our ken,
And there in glorious light discern,
  A band of Earth's true noblemen —
Adams, Monroe and Madison,
  And kindred Monticello's sage,
And he who led our armies on —
  The Hero of the Hermitage;
Deep-thoughted Webster, gallant Clay,
  And Calhoun, worthy triune band —
O, shall we see another day,
  When men like these shall guide the land?

Not in despair we close the page,
  Our country is destined to fill,
For Providence in every age
  Has shaped the nations to His will,
And out of all this chaos dire,
  Faith sees the upward rising morn,
When selfish schemers shall retire,
  And Freedom sanctified return.

A Happy New Year — patrons, friends,
A year to you of means to ends,
Brighter and better yet than all
It has been to your lot to fall.
To little children, with their eyes
Warm as the gleam of tropic skies;

To maidens fair, the loving, loved,
In all the grace of sex approved,
To woman with her meed of care,
To youth and manhood everywhere,
And age with hopes not anchored here,
The wish of many a glad New Year.

———

1878.

A buried year ! One more complete —
One more sealed up beyond recall —
Before Time's new born heir we greet,
'Tis well to muse how much of all
It brought to shape our life and hope,
How much of Memory's garnered store
Came to our lot within its scope,
That we should scan its record o'er.
Whate'er it holds of grief or joy,
Of light or shade, to mark its flight,
Reflective thought may find employ,
And profit if we read aright ;
For Time unravels mystery's skein.
Unfolds the problem dark at first,
Lifts and relieves the heavy strain
From hearts in sorrow long immersed.
The vessel, long by tempest tossed,
Glad spreads its wings to favoring gales,
And fading hopes or substance lost,
In time may find renewed avails.

" Unfading Hope," great boon of life,
Whose bow of promise ever spans
The rugged scenes of earthly strife,
And brightens e'en our humblest plans.
So came of old, in Palestine,
To chosen followers of the Lord,

The lesson of a love divine,
　　Their future steps to guide and guard ;
The shadow of the cross was flung
　　O'er Jesus, and His "hour had come,"
As came the words no mortal tongue
　　But His, could speak 'neath heaven's high dome —
" What I do, now thou knowest not,"
　　I tread a lonely pathway here,
But light shall bless your lowly lot —
　　" Hereafter " shall it all be clear.

O, bless'd " HEREAFTER," talisman
　　Not to Judean plains confined —
A gift in its far-reaching span
　　Embracing all of human kind:
To all there comes a trial hour,
　　Through which we only pass aright,
By seeking humbly for the power
　　To " walk by faith and not by sight."

The years in ever changeful tread,
　　Are mirrors to the thoughtful mind,
That " seeks the living 'mong the dead,"
　　Some consolation sweet to find:
Nor vain the quest, for treasured there
　　Are records we can ne'er forget,
Some blossoming seasons brightly where
　　The dew of morning lingers yet.

The thickest clouds but brief o'erspread
　　The joyful light of heaven's own blue,
And paths of conflict which we tread
　　Are but the mould of manhood true;
What though we fail to see the end,
　　When duty calls to painful work —
Not then before the Wrong to bend,
　　Not then the Right to basely shirk;

The victor's crown is poor indeed,
  Stained by a single flagrant wrong,
And justly hold this honored meed
  But few of all earth's worshipped throng;
The heroes on the shore of Time,
  Are not in self ambition bred —
Not made so on the fields of crime,
  Though such by fame oft heralded;
Obscure their station, all unknown
  Save by the One whose name is Love,
Their pathway often sad and lone,
  Like His, who marked the way above;
But though life's trial seasons now,
  May often cause the heart to bleed —
The "crown of thorns" still gird the brow,
  'Neath burdens borne for others' need —
Lose not the lesson of the past,
  Now speaking from departed days,
That sunny seasons overcast
  Came bright with joy's returning rays;
The future meet in hopeful trust,
  Each day in holy faith renewed,
Led by the promise "all things must
  Together work for highest good."

Bright be the New Year's gifts to you,
  Friends to whose doors we've daily come,
Its joys be many, griefs be few,
  That fall upon your earthly home;
Gather still closer in the way,
  That fosters in the household band,
The warm affections noblest play —
  Life's journey travel hand in hand.
Happy the lesson has been taught —
  "If solid happiness you prize,"
It need not far away be sought,
  "Within each breast the jewel lies."

16

A Happy New Year ! pause we now,
  Repeating thus the greeting old —
We backward look on what we know
  Ah ! who the future can unfold !
We know not what a day may bring,
  Much less our knowledge what a year,
The morning's brilliant coloring,
  In darkening clouds may disappear;
Or, all reversed, our fears at dawn
  May merge in peace and pleasantness,
Our sharp unrest be all withdrawn,
  A quiet calm our soul possess.
Imperial Time holds steady sway,
  In order close the days and weeks,
Bright eyes grow dim and locks turn gray,
  And change each living form bespeaks;
Be yours the portion, so that when,
  As now, December's latest day
Shall usher New Year's morn again,
  Life's brightest hopes may gild your way.